"Look," said Alix, a cold voice in the dark. "If you want to have this ridiculous conversation I will. We can pretend nothing's wrong, we can pretend we still want the same things. Would you like that? I tried as long as I could. I gave you the benefit of the doubt. But let's not play games, okay?"

"Don't you think we should talk about this?"

"We're past words now. Let's just go to sleep."

A thousand unspoken protests later Molly knew Alix was awake, even though neither of them had moved. Molly wished she could retreat into sleep, wished she could hear the ocean. She pictured it, this silent repetition of blue turning to white, swell to wave to spume, tumbling onto the beach, raking back, endlessly repeating its silent drumming. Facts of her life were thrown up on the sand, displayed, then erased by the tide, so that with each step she was forced to examine her options over and over. The waves posed one problem, cleared it, revealed another. Baby, no baby. The possibility of losing Alix, and losing New York. It didn't matter — the waves erased each one, leaving her a blank slate impossible to inscribe with any degree of certainty.

# STAYING HOME

## Elisabeth Nonas

The Naiad Press, Inc.
1994

Printed in the United States of America on acid-free paper
First Edition

Edited by Christine Cassidy
Cover design by Pat Tong and Bonnie Liss
   (Phoenix Graphics)
Typeset by Sandi Stancil

**Library of Congress Cataloging-in-Publication Data**

Nonas, Elisabeth, 1949–
    Staying home / by Elisabeth Nonas.
        p.        cm.
    ISBN 1-56280-076-0
    1. Lesbians—United States—Fiction.    I. Title.
PS3564.045S73    1994
813'.54—dc20                                                93-41449
                                                                    CIP

*For my father and for my sister*
*And for Carole (again and again and again)*

**Works by Elisabeth Nonas**

*For Keeps*
*A Room Full of Women*
*Staying Home*

# ACKNOWLEDGMENTS

While a novel is not a collaborative effort, a novelist needs various kinds of help as she writes. I would like to thank the following people for their time and valuable information: Jane Fantel and Jennifer Jackson talked to me about their process of becoming parents; Marki Knox, M.D. took an afternoon to explain for me the fine points of infertility, alternative insemination, and the potential problems involved; Roberta Bennett guided me through the legal side of adoption; and Michael Stevenson allowed me into his studio and answered all sorts of questions about what it is that art conservators do.

Once again Katherine Forrest provided insightful editorial comments that sent me back to the drawing board to come up with my own solutions.

Judith Branzburg read early drafts and made valuable suggestions along the way.

Susan Merzbach deserves thanks not just for reading and commenting on an early draft but for all kinds of support.

E. Marcy Dicterow-Vaj — thanks for the violin lesson.

My friend Pat Eliet was a tremendous support on my first two books. She talked with me when I was in the earliest stages of this one, often knowing before I did the themes I wanted to deal with, and helped me clarify the thoughts that later turned into characters and scenes. She died suddenly, before I was even close to a rough draft. Having had her with me through each of my novels, not to mention in my life outside writing, I really missed her on this one.

My lover / mate / friend / companion / partner/spouse (when is someone going to come up with a word for our tribe to use?) Carole Topalian started me on my first novel and has sustained me spiritually and emotionally through all of them. Every writer should be so blessed.

## About the Author

Elisabeth Nonas was born in New York City in 1949. In 1977 she moved to Los Angeles, where she lives with her lover, photographer Carole Topalian. She has written the screenplay adaptation of Paul Monette's novel *Afterlife*, articles for *The Advocate*, and is currently co-authoring with Simon LeVay a book on lesbian and gay life to be published in 1995 by MIT Press. She also teaches fiction writing at the Institute of Gay and Lesbian Education in West Hollywood and at UCLA Extension. She is the author of two previous novels published by Naiad Press, *For Keeps* and A Room Full of Women.

# CALIFORNIA

# MOLLY

Molly Rubin wished she had amnesia. Nothing massive, a selective variety would do. She didn't want to obliterate all her memories, not even the bad or painful ones. But her fear of the past's ability to influence the present told her that although she'd progressed steadily through her thirty-eight years, she had set her course early on. Maybe if she could forget who she'd been she could make herself a different person now.

Since she couldn't go back and change anything — not the little faux pas or the big embarrassments or the agonizing or frightening moments or the dread or the pressure or the loneliness — why couldn't she just forget? Hadn't she moved far enough away — three thousand miles, New York to Los Angeles — to avoid particular associations? Shouldn't time have dulled her susceptibility to the little smells or sounds that triggered each onslaught and transported her back so effectively as to make her lose her place in the present?

These days it seemed anything could set her off. Just that morning she'd put gas in the car, and the person paying in front of her — a guy with a Lakers cap on backwards and a Metallica T-shirt — popped a piece of bubble gum in his mouth, and from the smell alone Molly could taste the first gritty chews, feel the powder dissolve on her tongue, the sharp sweetness that stung the back of her throat and sometimes made her cough.

Back in ninth grade, midway through her first year in a new school, she and Sandy Stockwell — a sturdy girl who carried packs of bubble gum in her school bag, her books and papers reeked of Bazooka — had snuck down the back stairwell one Friday during recess.

"Again, Molly. And harder this time."

Molly took a deep breath, closed her eyes, balled up her fingers, keeping her thumb extended. She dropped her arm back as if swinging a bowling ball then flung it forward, thumb out, smack into the cinderblock wall. "Ow!"

"That looked better," Sandy Stockwell said. "What do you think?"

Sandy wasn't stuck up like a lot of the other girls in Molly's ninth grade class. She could have been, though. Her father Sander Stockwell — so many of these people had last names for first names, all those important families marrying each other —

had more money than anybody else's parents at the school, and that was saying something. Earlier that morning Molly had confided to Sandy that she was petrified about playing the guitar in a recital for the rest of the Upper School after recess. Molly had been practicing her piece for three weeks, knew it cold, but that didn't help her nerves any.

"If you jam your thumb you won't be able to play, right?"

So as soon as recess started Sandy had dragged her to the landing between the first floor and the basement.

After several halfhearted thrusts Molly's thumb was beginning to feel a little sore — or maybe she was just imagining it, since she had yet to really whack it head on.

"This is never going to work. It hurts a little, but it's not broken or anything. I don't even think it's sprained."

"Try it again. And concentrate."

Molly evaluated her options. She could continue to bang her thumb into the wall until Sandy was satisfied — and possibly do permanent damage to the digit — or go upstairs right now to Miss Pleasant, their teacher, and tell her she'd hurt it in volleyball and had to be excused from the recital. As long as she was going to lie — about the volleyball part — why tell the truth about the thumb?

Molly gingerly flexed her hand. "Mission accomplished," she said.

"Great." Sandy grinned, and they walked together up to see Miss Pleasant.

After the recital, Molly felt a little sorry that she

hadn't played. The girls who had performed glowed with accomplishment. Molly watched them being congratulated by friends and well-wishers.

Looking back on it, she wasn't so disturbed by the fact that she had lied or even that she had stooped to the tactic — just the opposite, since she'd usually been such a good, steady kid — it was the backing out at the last minute, even though she'd been prepared. What made her want to erase the memory was the ease with which she'd slipped out of her responsibility.

None of her musings were conducive to a productive morning. The September heat wave didn't help, either.

Living in the west end of the San Fernando Valley eliminated many of the distractions of L.A. proper, but the suburban house in the foothills of the Santa Monica Mountains offered its own diversions.

Squirrels scooted up trees, over the roof of the studio, feasted on green pine cones, littered the lawn with their discards. Circling turkey vultures cast eerie shadows that played on the grass and succulent-covered hillside. A red-tailed hawk screamed through the white-hot sky.

Each spring sparrows built nests under the eaves of the house. Lizards shed their skins on the steps down to the fruit trees. Compared to her life in Manhattan, Molly now lived in a PBS nature documentary. She must have spent five minutes watching Annie, their golden retriever, stalk the gopher hole before she finally shut herself in her workshop — actually a converted two-car garage designed to her specifications with work tables and skylights, a cross between a carpenter's shop and artist's studio and only a few steps from the house.

Sometimes she wished she'd picked a different profession, one that totally absorbed her mind and allowed no room for digression. Certain stages of her work as an art conservator were pleasantly mindless. Mindless didn't mean careless — she couldn't let her scalpel slip while she was scraping glue off the back of a canvas — but she'd been at this for almost fifteen years and could let her thoughts wander safely while she worked at certain tasks.

But what was safe? As Molly scraped away more dried glue, she wished she could scrape away the past that clung so tenaciously to her.

Alix always told her she thought too much, worried too much. And here she was again, worrying about the past, obsessing about getting out of that silly recital — no big deal. It hadn't meant anything at the time, and it didn't presage anything for the future. It's not like she was afraid of commitment. If she were, how could she have lasted eight years with the same woman — eight years of firm commitment to each other. Hadn't she proved that she was no shirker of responsibility, that she could be as dedicated as anyone? Hadn't she made a place for herself, a perfect fit?

Not that Molly suspected any of this lay in store for her when she first met Alix at a fancy reception given by one of the trustees of the county museum.

In the garden of a huge house in Pacific Palisades waiters and waitresses had silently passed hors d'oeuvres that Molly was calling dinner. The men were elegant in well-cut suits, the women in cocktail dresses, and Molly forever underdressed, a little uncomfortable.

She was sipping champagne and wondering how much time she had to put in before she could leave, when one of the guests approached and said to her, "I hate these things, don't you?"

Molly, not too interested in making polite cocktail conversation — although the woman was quite attractive in black crepe pants, black patent leather pumps, and white silk shirt — simply nodded.

A violinist strolled among the guests, stopping before couples or small groups to play sedate classical tunes. As he approached them Molly whispered, "How much do you have to tip him not to play for you?"

But it was too late, the musician was already there. He switched from classical to a devilish few bars of "Cheek to Cheek," winked at Alix, and moved on.

"Peace at last," Molly said. "So, do you work at the museum?"

"I'm a violinist."

"Right. Really, what do you do."

"Really. I'm with the band. Classically trained, but I do a lot of studio work, films, TV, commercials. An occasional party. I hired the musicians for this one."

Molly felt like a fool. "I'll just slink quietly off into the night."

"Without introducing yourself? I'm Alix Chase." She extended her hand.

Molly's gayometer had never been too reliable —

she often wished there was a lesbian password, some sure sign — but even she couldn't mistake Alix's grip or the direct intense hit from those baby blues.

After introductions, Alix asked what Molly did. Molly explained her work, then Alix said, "I want to hear more about this later. Don't go away." Alix left to take her place with the quartet that had just started to tune up.

That was the first time she heard her play. The performance mesmerized her. Many of the guests, too polite to continue conversing, stopped in their tracks, cocktails in hand, and silently gobbled hors d'oeuvres. Others near the bar set up at the far end of the patio kept talking. Alix seemed transformed, swept away by the music despite the informal setting. Or maybe, Molly realized in the middle of something she found out later was by Dvorák, she herself was the one transformed, swept away by the drama and the furious sliding of Alix's bow over the strings, her eyes closed at times, listening with some other part of herself, brought to the pure center of the music. Molly felt the heat of a blush on her cheek when she realized the effect this was having on her.

In their eight years together Molly had followed Alix all over town and beyond, watched her perform in high school auditoriums and theaters large and small, galleries, public halls, private homes. Alix became a stranger when she played — a mysterious presence, pure art. Molly, always delighted and amazed at the transformation, felt a thrill of pride each time she heard her, marveled that this woman, this talent, came home to her after every

9

performance, except of course for that first one. That night they had just gone out for coffee after the party.

The first night they slept together Alix had come over after a rehearsal. Molly had been listening to a Joni Mitchell tape. Alix took out her violin, tuned up and played along. Molly lost her heart then, no hope of recovery, and was carried into bed on the music — no corny jokes about being played like a violin, but every hope of just that occurrence fulfilled.

Molly dusted away the fragments she'd scraped loose. She stood and stretched, arching her back to work out the strain of hovering over the canvas. If she didn't find something that required more of her attention she'd spend the rest of the day scraping into her own past.

She stood in the doorway to stretch again. Luckily her studio stayed relatively cool. The dog had given up stalking, content to sprawl in the useless shade while squirrels and birds overran her turf. Too hot to bother.

A weak breeze teased the trees. Molly loved the eucalyptus this time of year. Their smooth trunks seemed to be made of clay, all the bark peeled off and lying in crisp pools at the base. They looked like sculptures of trees, a fantasist's image of a tree, its limbs impossible-to-believe shades of yellow, mauve, and gray.

Accustomed to shutting out the white noise of the

freeway a mile below, Molly picked up only the sounds around their property. Birds and squirrels chattering, the buzz of a small plane. Scales from Alix's violin drifted from the house, glided into Bach, warm-ups for her afternoon practice.

Molly turned back to her cool refuge, grateful for the variety of projects awaiting her attention. Broken sculptures and statues, bowls and little figurines, papers and panels and frames in various stages of repair and disrepair.

She reached for a ceramic Chinese horse. The small statue had been made into a lamp by its previous owner. People could be so careless, Molly thought. This piece of *ming chi* — tomb furniture, something the superstitious Chinese wouldn't buy at one point because of its association with death — had been left to its fate at the hands of Westerners who undervalued and impaled it, turned it into decorative art. Just taking out the pole for the bulb had restored most of the animal's dignity. Today she would remove any traces of old restorations.

"Never mind that you're twelve thousand years old," Molly said, dipping a cotton swab into ketone and carefully applying it to soften some old restorations. She almost wished the horse could talk, tell her about centuries past. Just as well, she thought, to let him have his own amnesia, mute and repairable, more perfect than her own.

She switched on the radio to NPR and spent the rest of the day working, listening to interviews and grounded in the present.

• • • • •

After dinner that night Molly doodled in the margins of a crossword puzzle. "What's a five-letter word for pith helmet?" Not that she expected an answer. She had stretched out on the bed to keep Alix company while she ironed.

"Shit!" Alix muttered for the thirtieth time as she pressed creases into rather than out of her shirt.

"That's only four letters." Molly closed her eyes. The creak and squeaks of the board, the pounce of the iron against it, the hiss of the steam all brought back vague early memories of being home from school. With Annie curled up next to the bed, it was all very cozy.

Another curse from Alix.

"I don't know why you bother," Molly said, "they're just going to get wrinkled in the. suitcase." She put down her puzzle. "Come here."

"I've got four more shirts."

Molly patted the bed and Alix sat reluctantly, curled in on herself. The dog rested her head on Alix's thigh, looked up at her with sad brown eyes. "She wants to get in on the act." Alix didn't crack a smile. Molly inched closer, put an arm around Alix's tensed shoulder, kissed her cheek.

Alix shrugged away. "Quit it."

Molly stroked Alix's shoulder. "It's only for a weekend. It'll be good for us."

"I hate these command performances. We're supposed to traipse all the way up there to pay homage to the newest member of the family who won't even know we're there."

"Don't you want to see her?" Alix's newest niece, Betsy, was by all accounts the brightest two-month-old ever. "Steve has been wanting you to come up ever since she was born."

"It's not like it's a rare occurrence," Alix snapped. Steve and Maddie had five children. "There's bound to be another any minute."

"Are you jealous?"

"Don't start with me, Molly."

"That's why you get so anxious every time they want us to come up."

"Molly, this is not open to discussion."

"I don't see why you don't just explain —"

"Not until I'm pregnant."

They'd been having the same argument for three years — ever since Alix had started being inseminated.

There lay the root of their problem — Alix's petulant reluctance to see her family, Molly's preoccupation with her past.

Once Alix got started she wouldn't let go. "I don't want to fight with them about this any earlier than I absolutely have to." She shot a spray of water at a sleeve, pounded the iron against the cotton. "I don't have to get their heterosexuality shoved in our faces one more time." Alix eyed Molly suspiciously. "And since when do you want to go see my family?"

The Chases had disowned Alix when she first told them she was a lesbian. It took years for them to come around to accepting her back into the family. Now, even though Molly and Alix were included in all family events, being around them made Molly claustrophobic. Everyone was nice enough to her now, but she remembered when Alix couldn't even mention her name to her family, couldn't even talk about the Unsinkable Molly Brown, or suggest a molly bolt for a hanging plant. Molly stayed on her best behavior around the Chases. Not that everything wasn't all right now, copacetic. Molly simply left an entire section of her life at home when they visited Alix's family. And since the Chases had moved to Oregon, every holiday and occasion had become a big deal; visits now involved the whole clan, required forethought, planes and reservations. More pressure for longer stays.

Molly wanted a genuine vacation with Alix, just the two of them for ten days or so, enough time to shake off the stress of work and baby-making and still have days left for relaxing. But she would content herself with a weekend in Oregon. Since someone else's baby would be the primary topic of their stay, Molly could pretend she and Alix were living their old life, before all the tests and delays and disappointments. If they couldn't have time alone because they each worked too hard and too long, then at least they could go to Oregon for a weekend and make believe.

She could act as if none of it had happened, that everything hadn't changed and wasn't about to. There lay the honest answer to Alix's question. Molly was suddenly willing to visit Alix's family because she needed a break from starting her own.

She filled in the last letter of her crossword. The author had built his puzzle around a Pasternak quote: "Man is born to live and not to prepare to live." Molly snorted. All she and Alix had done for the last three years had been to prepare. No living in sight.

Molly's father often told a story about his

wedding day. While he waited in his sharp captain's uniform (World War II had just ended), friends and family eagerly anticipating the radiant bride's march down the aisle, "Your grandfather turned to your mother and said, 'It's not too late to change your mind.'"

That became a family joke because of course Molly's mother had no intention of changing her mind. Ben and Claire's marriage lasted twenty-seven years, until Claire died — that's what made the story so sweet to Ben, the phrase so innocent.

Molly and Alix hadn't had a wedding, but had celebrated enough milestones to give Ben ample opportunity to offer his daughter the same out. "You can still change your mind," he said when she called to say Alix was moving in with her. Molly knew he said it with a smile. "It's not too late to get out of it," he reminded her before they signed escrow papers for their first house. She would chuckle and move steadily if cautiously ahead.

Oddly enough, he had nothing but encouragement about the baby. "I'll be a grandfather" had been his first reaction.

Where were all the cautionary voices, Molly wondered. Friends cheered them on; even her family was supportive. Why was she the only one who heard alarms?

Some internal timer ticking away ever since her evasion in ninth grade had suddenly sounded, and she battled against using the out she'd learned in that back stairwell, that her father had whispered to her any number of occasions, a family joke turned into a dormant mantra, jostled awake by the events of the past three years. Not until now did Molly realize that always in the back of her mind had been the dangerously liberating option that she could be out of there in a flash.

She hadn't put any of this together — the seemingly insignificant yet haunting memory of the recital, her wish for amnesia — until tonight. Suddenly the day's thoughts coalesced into a tight knot of memory that frightened her by revealing that her capacity to flee had been inside her all along. She had thought she'd found her place. She belonged here with Alix. And she'd thought nothing could change that. Until now. She realized that, like a cat on its ninth and final life, she had been saving her disappearing act for when she might really need it. To date nothing had challenged her position or the comfortable monotony of her life with Alix. But now, try as she might to avoid the conclusion, Molly had begun to hope that there never would be a baby.

One step off the small plane and Molly knew she would be hard put to have a moment to herself, let alone with Alix, over the weekend. A horde of Chases greeted them at the Medford airport. Betty and Tom Chase and their sons Jack and Steve were surrounded by an array of grandchildren — Jack's kids: Jack, Jr., Brian and Teddy; and three of Steve's: Tommy, Christie and Bill. The kids ranged in age from six to sixteen. They all looked alike — obscenely healthy and '50s all-American. The older boys shot up between visits so that Molly scarcely recognized them. Ruggedly handsome, no longer baby-faced, they were all long limbs and awkwardness. Even Christie, eleven and the lone girl, had grown, too fast for her, from the looks of it. She hung back from the others, her shoulders slightly hunched to hide what probably no one but herself would notice as breasts. And from the way Brian had eyed her and Alix at the gate, Molly suspected this twelve-year-old had also discovered breasts.

The Chases all had sturdy features and rough good looks. Alix possessed a delicacy that was more pronounced when she was away from them. But when she was thrown in with the others, being kissed and welcomed, the family resemblance was evident. They were all linked by the same dreamy blue eyes and pink cheeks.

Molly felt she stood out like a Hawaiian shirt on Wall Street. Her bright brown eyes and curly dark hair screamed ethnic, and no amount of California living could completely erase New York City from her accent or her appearance.

"Jean and Maddie are at the house with the baby," Alix's mother said, referring to Jack and Steve's wives. "Wait till you see her." She hugged her daughter, then Molly. A handsome sixty-plus, Betty Chase radiated good health and vitality. She was a fine match for Tom, who had a screen actor's good looks and an absent-minded professor's obliviousness to them. One glance at Betty revealed the source of the family's smile, teeth, and glowing complexion. The baby blues came directly from Tom.

The clan piled into the Chases' old Chevy Suburban. "How's everyone doing back there?" Alix's father glanced into the rearview mirror. He smiled at the chorus of "Fines" and started the ignition.

Molly and Alix each had a kid on her lap, as did Steve, Alix's oldest brother. Jack sat up front with his parents, and the rest of the gang piled into the back.

Car dealerships gave way to fruit orchards and then farmland. Molly had the oddest sense of being in an oversized New England state. The same landscape prevailed — rolling hills, mountains in the distance — but on a much larger scale than back East.

"I think we should go right to the game," Tom Chase said.

"Absolutely not," insisted Betty. "These girls haven't seen the baby yet."

"They're going to be here all weekend."

"They didn't come for football." Betty explained that it was the opening game of the season and Matt was in the starting lineup.

"I've been working with him on his blocking all summer," Tom pouted.

Betty patted his hand on the steering wheel. "Don't worry, you won't miss the game."

So motherhood won out over starting time and Tom Chase drove them grumpily to the house for their first glimpse of this perfection named Betsy.


Alix seemed reluctant at first to hold the baby. "I haven't washed my hands."

"Hurry up then," Maddie, the proud mother, said. "I've told her all about her famous Aunt Alix."

Crowded over the bathroom sink, Molly and Alix spoke to each other's reflection in the mirror.

"She's got Maddie's eyes," Alix said.

"Get out of here. All the kids look like your brothers. Or you. Any one of them could be yours." Alix's nieces and nephews looked like their fathers, with some reference to Maddie and Jean, but the Chase features dominated. Even at two months the baby's resemblance was remarkable, and there was no reason not to assume that Betsy wouldn't soon look like the others had as babies — tow-headed as the blond hills of Northern California in September.

"Maybe we'll kidnap this one. They've already got so many. Think anyone would miss her?"

"You'll have your own soon enough," Molly said out of habit, not convincing either of them. She shut off the faucet and shared a towel with Alix. "Ready?"

Alix leaned closer to the glass. "I look like shit." She pinched her cheeks to bring out a little color.

"You look fine. Quit stalling."

Alix heaved a huge sigh. "Okay. It's show time."

Alix held the baby so tenderly. The family oohed and aahed at each gurgle from Betsy, whose purple eyes glommed onto Alix's shape.

"I think she likes you," said Maddie.

"Of course she does, tell Mommy that," said Betty, wiggling Betsy's tiny hand with her finger. "And tell her auntie likes me too, doesn't she, yes."

Betty Chase smiled. Maddie smiled. Jack, Steve, and Tom smiled. Everyone beaming, beaming. That's all they did around the baby. Even Alix, between the few tears that leaked out, managed a weak grin.

"Isn't it just the most simple joy to watch a baby?" Betty asked.

Molly didn't think there was anything simple about it, at least not for her and Alix. She could be ours, Molly thought, ours will probably look like all these kids. Flooded with tenderness for Alix, with sympathy for the roller coaster of the last few years, Molly wanted to scream at the injustice of Alix's not having her own baby. Simultaneously her internal timer buzzed furiously. She almost looked for the door.

Maddie said, "Come on, Molly, your turn."

"Naw, she looks too happy with Alix."

"Don't be shy," Maddie urged, moving to take the bundle from Alix.

Molly gestured her to sit. "Really. Besides, I think I'm coming down with something."

Alix's father took this as his cue. "It's time to get to the game, anyway."

"Calm yourself," Betty said between coos over the baby. "The girls are probably hungry," she reminded her husband.

He looked at Alix and Molly. "They've got hot dogs there."

"Fine with me." Molly wasn't going to be the one to deprive him of the opportunity to watch his oldest grandson play the opening game of the season.

Despite Tom Chase's scooting along back roads and shortcuts, they missed the kickoff. The game had already started when they settled into their seats near the thirty-yard line. Tom sulked briefly but soon was too caught up in the plays to care about the few minutes he'd missed.

Molly had attended small private schools in New York City. The first one had no gym, much less teams to follow, and Cavanaugh had been all girls, so she had never been to a high school football game.

The crowd tonight was just as she had envisioned

21

it — parents and grandparents and siblings in family groups, groups of girls and blocks of boys surreptitiously eyeing each other, younger kids fooling around on the track that bordered the playing field, shooting paper planes at one another.

What she wasn't prepared for was the shock of the field, lit as bright and clear as their collective dreams. Everything appeared sharp and focused under the perfect velvet black sky. No stars yet — or perhaps they were there beyond the lights. But the stars would have been superfluous under that brilliant black. No one needed to make a wish. Who could have wanted more than this clarity?

The whole evening seemed like another time, another era. It calmed Molly just to look out toward the field. She knew nothing about football, so following the game was out of the question. And though she had no memories of her own, no moments like this in her past, she felt it might be possible to borrow something here, to concoct a memory of this spectacle and add it to her life, make it part of her history.

She watched for number 23, Alix's nephew Matt, and followed him, whether hurtling into an opponent or standing on the sidelines with his teammates, unself-conscious yet heroic with their exaggerated silhouettes — hulking padded shoulders balanced over tight narrow hips.

Tom and his sons eagerly followed the game, discussed the strong points of various players as if they were pros. They evaluated each play and the strategies involved. Everyone spoke fluent football. Even Betty Chase knew the basic rules and principles. Only Molly was in the dark. Had this been baseball she would at least have been able to follow along. But she didn't know a first down from a field goal. She watched Alix — usually her soulmate, her musical spirit, sensitive and gentle — howl with the rest of the crowd, leap up at certain plays, groan in disappointment at others. Maybe it came from growing up with brothers.

But Molly had grown up with a brother. Partly, anyway. He had died when she was eleven. Not learning to talk football had seemed the least of her deprivations, though it would have come in handy tonight. Past nights also, Molly confessed to herself, remembering other visits with the Chases.

She always watched Alix with her brothers, trying to learn something about how they communicated. Neither brother showed any musical aptitude, had no particular interest in the arts. They were accountants, strictly business, had nothing to do with Alix's world. Yet Alix could always predict their response to any incident — from politics to sports to family decisions.

Nothing in the present indicated their connection — if they weren't related they certainly wouldn't have been friends — yet always when they got together out would come stories about the time they dressed up the dog or dragged a mattress onto the driveway and spent the afternoon jumping off the roof of the garage.

Molly had become a student of these persistent, unalterable connections, ransacking her own past for similarities. But her link — her brother — was gone, and her stories with him.

During halftime she watched the cheerleaders. When they were finished, the drill team took the

23

field. Dressed as someone's ideal of femininity —
bright pink dresses with skirts that hung just below
the knee, with puffed shoulders and long sleeves,
bodice and sleeves sparkly under the lights — they
did no precision marching but rather a romantic
ballet to a pop ballad.

The croony music blared scratchily over the
loudspeakers as the girls swayed in unison. Molly
watched everything but her gaze returned constantly
to the sky, to that fabulous unreal black.

After the drill team the cheerleaders lined up
and encouraged the crowd to join them on the field.
Together they formed two parallel lines, an entryway
for the home team to charge through after halftime
ended. Some cheerleaders climbed onto each other's
shoulders. They worked the fans enthusiastically.

Alix said, "Cheerleaders were always my
favorites."

Steve joked, "Now we know why."

"Not because I'm gay," Alix said. "It had more to
do with their attitude."

"Sure," her brother said, "just like most men like
Dolly Parton for her music." He elbowed Jack and
winked. Alix just rolled her eyes.

Molly only half-listened. The pure blackness drew
her back to the field, where everything played in
bright relief against the infinite sky.

Alix leaned against her, a surreptitious contact
reserved for public and possibly hostile settings.

Molly had visited Japan with a friend she met in
graduate school. Taka invited her home to her
parents' house outside Tokyo. In the five weeks she
spent there, Molly marveled at the islands and
everything she visited, temples and rock gardens and

the shogun's castle with floors that squeaked so enemies couldn't surprise the guards. But she sensed the deepest mystery in the Ginza and the other bustling parts of Tokyo — on the surface as American as America but so profoundly different underneath that it didn't matter how many Big Macs or buckets of Kentucky Fried Chicken or blue jeans or T-shirts were sold. The contrast hung in the air, palpable but invisible. In any foreign country she'd visited up to that point, if she sat back and kept her mouth shut she could blend in, pass for a native. Molly couldn't pass in Japan. In the same way, she felt like a foreigner here. It wasn't just about being a lesbian in a crowd of heterosexuals. For all she understood she might as well be speaking another language. Her vocabulary wasn't up to this. Not just the football jargon, but the family and the togetherness, the spirit of the event.

Because of the setting or the sky or something else, these people out on the field and in the stands seemed different from their counterparts in L.A. or New York. Not because of the clichéd innocence of the small town — Molly knew that in their real lives they watched the same television shows and hated or loved the same politicians, experienced the same betrayals. But tonight wasn't real life. Under this clear black dome they all belonged to a particular vision that no longer existed for Molly: the closeness of family, and of belonging to something.

Matt's team won, 23-7. The Chases celebrated with ice cream and cake at home. The cozy living room swarmed with kids and adults all talking about the game and school and the plans for the rest of the weekend and wanting to be sure Alix saw this or came here or just paid attention. Tom specialized in magic tricks, and gathered everyone to watch him cut pieces of rope and have them miraculously come together again. When he pulled coins out of Christie's ears, she blushed and begged him to teach her how to do it.

"Do what?" he said. "I don't *do* anything, I just reach in like this —" He buried his hand in her ponytail — "and pull out whatever I find. Like this quarter. You should brush your hair more often, you'd be rich." The kids laughed and Christie blushed again.

Maddie and Jean had driven over and, between lullabies to quiet the baby and interruptions of game reports from their children, asked what Alix had been up to since the last visit. Steve, wrestling with Brian and Jack, Jr., rolled over onto a bowl of popcorn. Betty Chase laughed along with everyone else. She didn't even seem bothered when Tommy spilled his ice cream on the rug. She just sent one of the other kids for a towel.

Molly's family had never been anything like this. She couldn't even imagine an equivalent. She might as well have been on the moon for all she understood of this kind of life.

In bed later she curled behind Alix. "You sleeping?"

"Almost," Alix murmured.

The sky had returned to its starry state, millions of holes poked through that fabulous black. Molly imagined herself with Alix on the field, that sharp dark above them. She kissed the back of her neck. "You used to do that rope trick for me, remember?" Early on, Alix had enchanted her with tricks her father had taught her. Molly slid her hand down Alix's side, across her stomach. "Let's work some magic now."

Alix muttered some excuse and stilled Molly's hand.

Molly didn't push her luck. She knew from past visits that Alix wrapped herself in images of Betsy or any baby like a second skin, impenetrable. Molly rolled onto her back, arms behind her head.

Ever since Baby had become primary in their lives, Molly longed for a hint of the passion that had sparked between them earlier. She wanted to be someone else, someone hot and romantic. Someone who'd throw Alix down on the bed, or shove her up against a wall, or onto the rug or a table or someplace other than the bed—Alix on the right always, Molly on the left always, one first then the other, or both at once, but always, always, always the same. Not bad, not completely unsatisfying, but the same.

Tonight Molly would have settled for the sameness.

The rest of the weekend passed in a whirl of people and activity. Breakfasts were reasonably quiet, consisting of just the four of them — Alix's parents and Molly and Alix. Every other moment was filled with Family. Every meal, every waking hour. Alix's brothers brought the kids over at nine-thirty Saturday morning and that was it for the day. Maddie sat with Betsy asleep in her lap and everyone watched that tableau for at least half an hour. Then the whole clan piled into and out of the huge Chevy to visit pear orchards. They lumbered down quiet roads or barreled down the Interstate in search of panoramic views and scenic hikes, the best spot for a picnic.

On one of the outings Molly and Alix ended up miraculously alone on a wooded trail. When they'd first stepped out of the car Molly thought they must be near a main road because she heard the whoosh of traffic.

Alix said, "Listen to that." Everyone quieted down. Jack, Jr. complained he didn't hear anything but the wind in the trees. "That's what I wanted you to hear," Alix said.

They all stood there — Alix and Molly with Tom, Betty, Jack, Jean, Brian, Jack, Jr., Teddy, Steve, Maddie with Betsy strapped across her chest, Tommy, Christie, Bill, even Matt had come along today — listening to the wind in an ocean of trees. No sound but the wind and an occasional crunch in the dirt when someone shifted balance (probably one of the boys growing, Molly thought). Molly looked out over miles of forest — decades, centuries, of trees. Time made visible and audible. The kids probably didn't get it, but Molly let the whisper blow through her, hoping some of its peace would stick.

They started hiking up a trail but within minutes their merry band had dispersed and Molly marveled at finding herself alone with Alix in the midst of this green splendor.

Alix must have felt the same way because she

looked around and flung herself into Molly's arms. "I miss you."

"We've been together every minute since we left L.A."

"But it's not the same," said Alix, locking her fingers in Molly's curls and kissing her neck. "I could make love to you right here."

One part of Molly scanned the area for a rock to hide behind, the other stayed on the lookout for Family.

"Are you having a good time?" Alix asked.

"Sure. How about you?"

"Yes. I mean really in a big way yes." Alix leaned into her again. "I'd like to raise our baby somewhere like this," she whispered into Molly's ear.

For a nanosecond Molly thought it might just be possible. There was something very seductive about the idea — she saw a flash of that black sky — but not at all realistic. "What do we live on — pears?"

"I'm serious."

"So am I," Molly said, disengaging from Alix's arms.

"You can't even let yourself pretend for a minute."

"Sure I can."

"Then couldn't you imagine living somewhere like this, you and me and the baby?"

If Molly set this picture up in her mind's eye it would mean admitting the possibility of Baby, accepting one part of the premise as reality, then making the leap to fantasy. Alix was like a good salesperson who almost convinced you to spend an extra twenty dollars on the two-year warranty — it's a much better value, they assure you — when in the first place you really had no interest in the one-year warranty.

"Would it be so terrible?" Alix persisted.

"What's the point? Neither of us could make a living up here."

Alix stroked Molly's cheek. "Where's the harm in a little make-believe?"

A crunch and a giggle in the woods behind them signaled someone's arrival. Alix stepped back just as Christie and Brian crashed through the brush. "Lunch is ready," they announced joyfully.

Molly kicked herself for the rest of the day. Once again she'd spoken too quickly. Why should she fight over where they'd live when the baby came when she didn't believe that there ever would be a baby?

A blur of Chases took Molly and Alix to the airport on Sunday afternoon. Betty Chase pressed a tin of freshly baked cookies into Molly's hands, everyone said goodbye and waved, and then they were in their seats.

The plane heaved into the same sky that had covered the game, blue now, though Molly knew its potential for perfect black. Within a day or two they'd be ensconced in their real lives, as if the trip and that sky had never happened at all.

Three days later Molly wasn't ensconced in anything. What had she been thinking. She and Alix didn't have a real life anymore. They had been hovering in uncertainty for three years. They followed no set routine; everything was anticipation. For three years they'd lived under the assumption that their lives could change radically at any moment — or, to be technically correct, any menstrual cycle.

Molly sat in her studio at nine-thirty in the morning with all the windows and door and skylight open to catch any breeze that might stir the heavy heat they'd lived with since they got back. It would be over a hundred again, she thought. She stared at an oxblood vase she had pieced together from shattered remains. She had wanted to airbrush over her work but in this heat the acetone dried too quickly and the vase would have to wait until the heat broke.

The delay frustrated her, though no more so than her own naiveté. To think they'd be ensconced in their real life — ha.

The moment the plane lifted off, Oregon becoming a lush green miniature below them, Alix had turned to her and said "Well, we did that," and spent the rest of the flight looking out the window.

Just like that, their weekend was dismissed as if nothing counted for Alix unless it went directly toward baby. Their life used to be a delightful and scattered affair — varied, spontaneous and filled with friends. Now it was a single-minded drive: everything had to have something to do with Baby.

As if on cue, Alix walked into the studio and announced "I'm ovulating. Norma can take me at two. Can you be ready to leave at one-thirty?"

"But that's when the movie starts. Can't you go earlier?" One of Molly's favorite things was to duck out of work for a few hours to catch a matinee, sit in the dark holding hands with Alix, like old times.

The first time she'd told Alix she loved her had been at a movie. Molly had stared at her for so long that Alix finally turned to her. "What?" Not like she didn't know, because she must have, the way Molly's eyes filled with tears. No words necessary but Molly had said it anyway — "I love you."

"Look, you can go to the movie without me."

"That's not the point," Molly said. "We had plans."

"The movie plays every day. I don't ovulate every

day. Do we have to fight each time? This isn't going to go on forever."

"How long then?" Molly challenged.

"I've already told you — just a few more inseminations."

"Then what?" Molly demanded.

"Then we'll talk about the next step."

Molly didn't say anything. She couldn't bring herself to tell Alix that she might not want this baby. She brought out her palette and brushes. She could work on the Tang horse; the heat wouldn't affect that.

"So are you going to come with me?" Alix didn't let Molly answer before saying, "We could go to the five o'clock show, grab a bite after. Please."

Alix leaned over Molly's shoulder, brushed her ear with her lips, raising bumps up Molly's arm and an electric jolt between her legs. "You don't mean this," Molly said, tilting her head to allow Alix's lips access to her neck.

"Oh, yeah?" Alix's hands snuck under Molly's shirt.

Molly looked at the Tang horse. Too much heat for anything now. She leaned back into Alix. "I have to meet a client at noon, but I can be back in time for your appointment." She swiveled her chair around, drew Alix onto her lap. She was a sucker for seduction.


They'd talked about babies ever since they'd first met, but the topic hadn't come up for real until they'd been together for five years. One romantic rainy afternoon after making love they lay in bed listening to the rain on the roof and watching the sky darken. Each made suggestions — we should light a fire, we should make dinner, we should order Chinese, go out for pizza — and neither moved, too warm and close and lazy after sex. They turned to each other. Molly's hand roamed Alix's side, stroked her face, began a steady descent.

Molly said, "I can't seem to get enough of you." She closed her eyes, buried her face in Alix's neck. They'd made love so many times already that afternoon that Molly was surprised at the intensity of her excitement now. "Tell me what you want," she whispered.

"I want us to make a baby."

Molly thought Alix was joking. "I mean something we could do right now."

"That's what I want," Alix said.

Molly wasn't sure how to take this. "Well, maybe if we keep at it —"

Alix rolled away, turning her back to Molly.

"Aw, baby . . . Alix . . . come on. I was just kidding."

"But I wasn't. I know we can't do it on our own, but the idea — I was serious."

"I know."

"Then why'd you say that?"

"It was just a joke. I'm sorry." Molly curled behind Alix, who shrugged her away. Molly kissed Alix's back, tongued around her spine.

"Leave me alone."

"I can't."

"Try."

Molly lay still a moment. Images played in her mind — Alix pregnant, Molly holding her baby, the two of them watching the baby's first steps. "Alix, talk to me."

Alix turned to face her. By now what gray light the storm had provided was practically gone. The rain had passed. Some clouds lingered against an intense blue sky, royal mixed with turquoise, deep and infinite. Molly could barely make out her lover's face. Alix took Molly's hand, guided it inside her again.

Molly closed her eyes as her fingers entered this smoothest, softest place. She imagined it the same color as the darkening sky, as deep and as infinite.

Alix pressed Molly's hand. She said, "If it were possible, I'd already be pregnant." She tightened around Molly's fingers. "I love you."

Molly would have given Alix anything.

Two days later Alix had called her gynecologist.

Lynn and Dory were also trying to get pregnant when Alix started. Lynn had talked an old boyfriend of hers into being a donor. She was using a turkey baster to impregnate Dory.

Molly and Alix were doing all this through sperm banks and had talked to Carla, an attorney (and mother, with Janey, of Nicholas), about drawing up papers defining everyone's relationship to everyone else. Ultimately Molly would adopt the baby, who would then have two legal mothers.

"But what about the donor's rights to the baby?" Molly asked Lynn.

"You mean Jack? He's cool. He's not the father type. But he has the greatest bone structure."

Molly figured that Dory and Lynn's method

would have saved them many thousands of dollars. This cost so much more than Molly had anticipated — who could have imagined all the possibilities afforded by new technology? Molly added each insemination, each ultrasound, each ovulation prediction kit to the running total in her head.

And neither she nor Alix had figured in the time or the complications. Alix's basic blood workup to test her endocrine functions revealed a thyroid problem that was brought under control in three months. But those were three months of no inseminations. Luckily they coincided with the four months she'd had to wait for the rubella vaccine to take. When the first six months of inseminations yielded no results, Alix underwent more tests: laproscopy, hysterosalpingogram. Diagnosis: endometriosis. Eight months of steroids took care of that. Two months later she was back in the saddle, or stirrups, again.

Each procedure became another war story for Alix to swap with Lynn and Dory, Amanda and Kayla, Carla and Janey.

But none of it deterred Alix. Not the discomfort, the disappointment, not even the cost. She took every call for work, played double sessions. Then she came home one day and announced she had sold the beautiful old French violin her parents had given her when she was accepted to Julliard. She replaced it with a newer Italian instrument.

"How could you do that?" Molly asked. "You always said the Viaume was priceless."

"I was wrong."

"But you loved it."

"It was only a violin, Moll, wood and silver-wound gut. It's not such a big deal. Plus, I made twenty thousand dollars on it."

But for what? To hear others boast of their fertility? By the second year of Alix's trying Lynn and Dory had their son, Jason. "Can you believe she got pregnant the second try?" Lynn crowed. "We hope it's as easy with our next one."

Amanda, after trying for a year, gave up on getting pregnant and started adoption procedures. She and Kayla now had their daughter, Gail.

Those couples would invite Molly and Alix over for an evening of baby-watching, baby stories, hope and encouragement. *Don't give up. It'll happen for you. Be patient.*

Even more friends had started with inseminations and adoptions. Pictures of fetal ultrasounds were stuck on refrigerators of lesbians all over L.A. At parties, instead of talking about the hottest bars or the best cocaine (early '80s talk), or swapping numbers of plumbers and contractors (late '80s), they shared pediatricians' numbers, information about play groups and preschools. At least the others did. Alix got only sympathy.

Molly didn't know how she kept going. She debated with herself about giving Alix an ultimatum: this better be the last time or else.

Or else what? Molly didn't want to think about that.

# *Alix*

Molly doesn't think I feel passion anymore. That's all I feel these days. The passion for a child — how can she expect me to weigh anything against it? Pros and cons — what con could stand against the reality of Baby, the soft helpless need and love?

My passion for Molly is undiminished. She doesn't think I know what she's going through. Compared to where I started, I know so much.

Here's what I knew when I went to Julliard: music. And my violin. I knew it snug under my chin, the depths I could see into the warm polished wood, the calluses on my fingertips (my own wooden veneer, my instrument extending to my body, or my body conforming to the instrument). I knew the days I could coax the highest saddest notes from its thin belly. Or from my own deep longing for something I couldn't define but that spoke to me through music.

I didn't know New York City. Having grown up in Los Angeles, I believed that if the sun was shining it would be warm out. I didn't know about winter. Or about men. I knew about California surfer boys, my brothers and their friends. And the few guys I had dated from my high school, the brainy types.

Not that this mattered. I didn't have to know anything else but music for my first year at Julliard. Laura introduced me to what I know now.

Laura had come from Boston. She wasn't enrolled at the school but knew everyone there, hung out a lot. She was thinking of applying. She was a brilliant pianist, and we played duets together. She introduced me to New York. Not just the buses and subways and Central Park and the museums but Katherine Hepburn double features at the Regency. We'd buy pound cake and tea at the coffee shop on the corner and spend the afternoon at the movies.

Laura lived in a studio apartment in a brownstone on the Upper West Side. She didn't have furniture, only unpacked moving boxes, a mattress on the floor, and a piano. But way before we got to the mattress we stood in her kitchen one evening after *Bringing Up Baby* and *The Philadelphia Story* and then — I swear I didn't know it was coming — she was kissing me, and to my infinite surprise and wonderment, I was kissing her too and she shoved me against the counter, or I let myself be shoved because who could resist. I hadn't felt anything like that since music, that same previously undefined longing suddenly understood not by my brain but by my hands. The callused fingers of my left hand playing up her spine were unable to accurately read the softness so I followed closely with my other hand, translating as it went, feathering up vertebra by vertebra, planing over to her back and then to her shoulder, down her side, and to the incredible soft weight of her breasts. My left hand rough and dense but even those blind wooden fingers suddenly sensate and knowing.

We kissed, tongues swirling. Dizzy with feeling I heard myself utter sounds I'd never made before but that were connected to music, to the feeling of music, to the inarticulate thoughts and sensations that become music.

Laura lifted me onto the counter — I had never known women could be so strong — pushed up my skirt and pulled down my pantyhose, plunged her fingers inside me and I was gone. Head pressed back against the cupboards I pulled her to me, slid my lower body toward her. She carried me to that mattress in the middle of the room and I don't remember much else about the next three weeks except the dark blue sheets, coffee cups on the packing boxes, meals eaten as we sat propped against the wall, no meal uninterrupted by sex.

There was music then, too. Long passages of Vaughn Williams instead of conversation. Elgar, Beethoven, Dvorák and back to bed.

After that I understood the city better. And music, too. But for the duration I was simply breathless. Breathless for three weeks. That's all it lasted. Laura left New York after that, went back to

Boston to the Berkeley School of Music. She never even unpacked her boxes.

We had never spoken of love, of women in love, of men, never pretended we'd go back to men or settle for men or deny what happened between us. We simply existed in that little room.

I couldn't say I missed her when she left. I wanted my breath back. I wanted to go at my own pace instead of Laura's constant high intensity.

After she moved I went numb for a time. My overloaded senses screeched to a halt. For three weeks I didn't pick up my violin because I thought I understood music, understood and therefore no longer had to play or learn about it. But passion cannot be stilled for long. I took out my violin, polished the smooth wood until I could see myself reflected in the soundboard. Soon I was practicing again.

Balance restored, I emerged from my isolation and reimmersed myself in my studies.

I wrote home once a week. My parents came to New York the next fall. We saw one Broadway play, *A Chorus Line,* two concerts at Julliard, and took a Circle Line boat tour around Manhattan. I introduced them to a new friend of mine, Jonathan. They took a liking to him, kept referring to him in their letters to me, thought of him as my boyfriend. Which he eventually became. More than that, we actually got married. I was young and didn't know. After Laura I let my passion for music mask everything else.

I didn't sleep with a woman again for eight years. The saddest thing is, I didn't think I missed it, either.

• • • • •

My marriage to Jonathan didn't last very long.
Shouldn't have happened at all, but in those days I
couldn't see — wouldn't let myself see — what I really
wanted.

Jonathan wanted babies. He'd bring me flowers
and wine, massage my back until I wanted him and
then try to sweet-talk me into not going for my
diaphragm, or not insisting he wear a condom — just
this once, he'd urge. I'd plead career, I'd wail for
music. It was my life, I insisted. Wait, I would say,
wait until. There was always a concert or an
audition. Soon I had recording sessions. We had
visits from my parents, from his. Always some
excuse or other. It didn't matter to me. I would use
anything. And then I met Jane.

For eight years I hadn't needed, hadn't noticed,
hadn't lacked. I existed with my music and with
Jonathan. Jane house-sat for Cathy, our neighbor
down the hall, an actress who had just been cast in
her first film and was off to L.A. for a couple of
months.

Jane worked in a bank and she was going
through a bad divorce, Cathy told me one day as we
waited for the elevator together. "I needed someone
to take care of Barrymore while I'm gone, and Jane
needs a place to think, not to mention sleep. You'll
like her."

Barrymore was a spoiled Abyssinian who devoted
its nine lives to escaping from Cathy's apartment.
Sometimes I would step into the hallway and the cat
would be slinking along the wall, delighted with
itself for managing this limited freedom. I'd ring

42

Cathy's bell then ring for the elevator. "Barrymore" was all I had to say, and Cathy would rush out and scoop him up before the elevator opened and he'd have a chance to get into some real trouble.

I do believe in fate. Something greater than myself. Call it what you will. Coincidence. Destiny. Everything happens for a reason.

I had just bagged the kitchen trash and stepped into the hallway to dump it in the canister by the service elevator. A sleek brown blur flew past me. Once in our apartment, Barrymore was next to impossible to coax out. I went for reinforcements.

Cathy's door was propped open by a bag of groceries. I knocked. I heard a woman's voice talking on the phone. Not Cathy's voice, but that of an unhappy woman. "Don't you understand it's too hard to see you? Please don't call again. I'm hanging up now." I heard her cradle the receiver. I heard her crying.

I didn't want to intrude on this moment and was about to retreat when she came to the door. Business suit, shirt unbuttoned, one earring on, one in her hand, stockinged feet.

"I'm really sorry . . ." I trailed off.

She hastily wiped her eyes, tried to do something about her appearance, at least tuck in her shirt. She gave up, though.

I introduced myself.

Jane nodded. "Seven-B. Cathy told me about you." She shook my hand then stooped to pick up her groceries.

The sadness in her eyes, in her posture — even her hair seemed tired — made me envy this woman. I didn't want her pain, but I wanted to feel so much for someone that I would have the potential for that great a loss. I wanted my love to count for something.

"Barrymore's out," I said.

She'd clearly forgotten all about him. "Oh, God. Did he get in the elevator?"

"He's in my apartment. It's not a problem for me but my husband's really allergic."

Jane dumped the groceries inside the apartment, shut the door, then followed me down the hall. It took us fifteen minutes to corner Barrymore and another five to lure him out of Jonathan's corner of the closet.

"I'm not going to tell him," I said. "If he knew, he'd be sneezing for days."

Jane apologized for letting the cat out, then left. Twenty seconds later, Barrymore still tucked safe under her arm, she was back. "I seemed to have locked myself out. Does the super have a key?"

Jonathan and I had one, so I let Jane and Barrymore back in.

Two days later she slid a note under our door inviting us for a drink that evening. Jonathan was teaching every night so I went alone.

Cathy had mentioned Jane's divorce. She hadn't mentioned that Jane's marriage had been to another woman.

That night Jane talked about Roberta and I listened. They had been together for three years. Roberta had fallen in love, or in lust, with someone else. Jane wanted to work things out. Roberta couldn't see past this other woman.

We talked every night after Jane got home. She'd come to our apartment, or I'd go to hers. I told Jane about Laura, the first time I'd spoken about her to anyone.

A few days later was a bank holiday, President's Day or something, and I suggested we go to a Katherine Hepburn double feature, *Pat and Mike* and *Adam's Rib*. We bought pound cake and tea at the coffee shop on the corner. As we walked home Jane put her arm through mine and we bent into the cold wind together. When we stepped into the elevator Jane pressed the button for our floor and asked if I'd like to come up for the usual.

"I don't care about the drink," I said. I moved to her, touched her face with my right hand, took her right hand with my left.

"I don't know about this," she said.

"Please," I said. My fingertips pressed against her cheek, red and cold from the wind. She would want to argue fairness, to me, to Jonathan. She would want to tell me about her unresolved feelings for Roberta. I covered her lips with my own to prevent her from speaking.

I didn't close my eyes while we kissed. Her eyelids fluttered down, thick lashes blurring. Her face my world that moment.

She didn't fumble for her keys. We left a trail of clothes into the bedroom. I made her leave on a dim light in the corner. I needed to see. She made one last protestation: was I sure I knew what I was doing. Again I kissed her quiet.

And I watched: my hands on Jane's body; the marks of my fingers on Jane's flesh; the confused look in her eyes when I entered her — Pleasure with me and the longing for Roberta: glad for this, sad for that.

I made love to her so she could forget. I made love to her so I could remember.

I didn't close my eyes until halfway through my coming.

One day I was called for a last-minute recording session. I made it back to Jane barely half an hour before Jonathan was due home. We didn't even make it to the bedroom. She opened the door and I was at her, yanking her shirt out of her pants, tugging at her zipper. She pulled us to the floor between the couch and the wing chair. We never even undressed.

That night Jonathan and I sat on our couch reading. He laid his head in my lap and started to talk about his day. After five minutes he started to sneeze, and his eyes teared up. He went for Kleenex. "If I didn't know better I'd swear there was a cat in here."

After that I would change my clothes when I came home from being with Jane.

We saw each other every day for seven weeks, until Cathy came back from L.A. Jane would still be staying in the apartment, but our meetings would probably end.

I had no illusions about what I was for Jane. I had no illusions about anything. Once I admitted to myself that I loved Jane, and I did love her for how she made me feel, for how she touched me, for making me realize what I really wanted, I knew I couldn't stay with Jonathan any longer.

I had kept my eyes open as much as possible,

thrilled at my capacity to see. Suddenly everything was in sharp focus, like when the eye doctor adjusts your prescription and each new diopter makes the chart clearer, the letters sharper, the outlines crisper. The world was new to me.

Not until I started seeing again did I realize I had stopped for eight years. Blinders off now, myopia corrected, I looked at women. On the streets, on buses, in rehearsals. Hailing a taxi, picking up a head of lettuce in the market. Every night I closed my exhausted eyes, weary from seeing, and gave thanks for the beauty and strength and variety of women in the world.

I was honest with myself but not with everyone else at first. I did not tell Jonathan I was a lesbian. I blamed our divorce on everything but that, on our difference about having a baby (though I knew I wanted one and suddenly understood why I'd been reluctant with him), and on New York — he was a native, I missed California.

I moved back to Los Angeles. I stayed with my parents for two weeks until I found my own apartment in Hollywood. They were very supportive of me despite their fondness for Jonathan. I did not tell them the real reason for the divorce.

I kept my social life separate from my family life. Once I'd had my vision corrected, I had little trouble meeting women. I'd been living in Los Angeles for two years when I spotted Molly at that party. I knew right away. I played for her that night. I tucked my violin under my chin and spoke to her through it, with words I'd never have, never know, and never need.

After we'd been going out for a few months I picked Molly up at her studio, which at the time was a rented garage and garage apartment behind a house in North Hollywood. Sometimes she pulled a table outside and worked in the driveway, and on this day I came upon her absorbed in piecing together an old porcelain teacup. The sun picked up the reddish highlights in her darkest brown hair as she bent over her work. She handled the delicate pieces — there must have been twelve of them — with such competence, gentle yet firm. Lost in her task, the tip of her tongue between her lips as if that somehow steadied her hands. She looked as she must have when she was a kid, possessed of that same intense concentration, yet with more patience than any child could manage. The perfect combination in a parent, I thought.

But those early days were not the time for Baby.

I had never been so happy. I neglected my career for a few months, too wrapped up in this woman, in myself and what I was feeling. When I finally moved back into my real life, Molly was an integral part of it. I'd never known compatibility and passion to continue for so long. After five years together, on my thirtieth birthday, I cried because my life was so good. I lived with the woman of my dreams and with my music. I couldn't have asked for more.

Then one day out of nowhere, a few weeks later,

I'm driving by Griffith Park and see a mother hand her child an ice cream. No big deal. No intimate moment. But every sliver of thought or urge I'd ever had for baby crystallized into that gesture. You can only leave two things behind when you die: children and art. My music is personal, mine. Others hear it, but it is not my legacy. I want to leave something to the world, a new voice and a new spirit. When I saw that woman lean toward her child I knew I was ready to get started.

I thought we were ready.

Molly resisted me on Baby from the beginning, even when she seemed almost happy about it. I could then understand Jonathan's frustration with me. I remembered his back rubs, the flowers and wine. No way I could trick Molly into this the way Jonathan had tried to with me. But I believed she'd be such a good mother, and like it so much, that she'd forget her reluctance as soon as she saw Baby.

I hadn't counted on the delays, the difficulty of getting pregnant.

But I remember my eight years of living monochrome, married to a man I liked but believe I was constitutionally incapable of truly loving. I will never again compromise on what is important to me.

Molly's agreeing to come with me to the doctor is a sign. Maybe her presence will change my luck. Maybe I can't get pregnant until I know she wants this as much as I do.

How can she not see my insistence on her involvement as a sign of my passion?

# *Molly*

Molly cursed. Not even rush hour, and aleady traffic on the Ventura Freeway was backed up for miles. Bumper to bumper in the steaming September heat wave. A glaze of heat bleached the scenery. Molly had shut off the truck's air conditioning and opened all the windows. Her eyes flicked nervously from the road to the temperature gauge hovering near red. She prayed the engine wouldn't overheat — they couldn't afford a major repair bill.

She yanked impatiently at her seatbelt. A trickle of sweat rolled down her stomach. A damp circle had formed on her shirt between her breasts where the strap pressed against her. She was due home in fifteen minutes and the last mile had taken her longer than that. Even without traffic she was fifteen minutes from her exit. Alix was going to be pissed.

She should have just canceled her meeting. She usually had her clients come to her. Her time was best spent on her work, not commuting, but she made an exception for Mrs. Falk, an old lady who didn't drive. Mrs. Falk loved her treasures, and loved to talk about each acquisition, where she and the late Mr. Falk had found each piece in their collection. Molly had tried for twenty minutes to get away before she was finally in her car. She'd made great time until she hit this stretch. She hadn't moved in the last five minutes.

The heat made Molly think back to when she was five and went with her family to Bermuda for Christmas vacation. Today's hot gusts brought back the shock of her first steps onto a tropical runway, walking toward a terminal open to the trade winds. Palm trees whispered everywhere, strange and exotic. At first the winds had scared her, and she'd slid her hand into her older brother's for reassurance.

She could use some outside reassurance now. She and Alix were not much help to each other.

During all the craziness after Alix came out to her parents, Molly and Alix had gone to Hawaii for a week. They rented a house on Kauai, right on the beach, ate papaya for breakfast and lunch, helicoptered through a spectacular canyon, went out in Zodiacs to the Nepali coast, lay on white sand beaches. But the most spectacular memory she had was of making love with Alix in the middle of the night, turning to her without words, listening to their own breathing and moans and the waves against the beach. The surf seemed louder at night, traveling across the smooth sand like music.

Their troubles with Alix's family had brought them closer together, fortified their love. These days nothing seemed to bring them close, forget closer.

Molly could no longer tell if the heat came from inside or outside herself. She had no recall of other weather, of winter rains or cool foggy mornings. Even after twelve years in L.A., the harsh, untamed quality of the Valley weather still surprised her. Ten or fifteen degrees hotter than the rest of the L.A. basin, this uncivilized heat belonged in the desert, in some uninhabited, uninhabitable location, not a densely populated suburb crowded with tract houses, mini-malls, yogurt parlors and nail salons.

Molly didn't like living in the Valley. It was too straight, too suburban. She missed their Silver Lake house, the neighborhood with its ethnic mix and sense of self. They had moved for the baby — everything they did was for the baby. Molly had wanted to look in Santa Monica. The air's better, she kept telling Alix, better for the baby. But Alix had kept dragging them farther and farther into the San Fernando Valley, where they would get more house for their money.

The woman in the next car applied mascara as she inched along. The guy in the Porsche in front of Molly had been leaning on his horn ever since a white Escort cut in front of him. As if this personal vendetta mattered — no one was going anywhere. There was an accident on the other side of the freeway, going toward L.A. Up ahead, red lights flashed.

*If we still lived in town I wouldn't have to fight this mess.*

Molly turned on the radio. She hit scan, which suited her mood. Five seconds per station — the intelligent, modulated tones of an NPR interview skipped into a few brassy bars of something baroque which were cut into by whiny country interrupted by an urgent "Praise Jesus," no segue to wailing Led Zeppelin on classic rock. The guy in the Porsche still leaned on his horn. *What a jerk.* The Escort driver flipped him off. He was a jerk too. A mellow rock station told her their music was right for whatever she was doing.

Traffic started to move. By now Molly was half an hour late. She braced herself for Alix's anger and stepped on the gas.

Even in the blackest of moods Molly had to admit their house had a certain charm, "curb appeal," the real estate agent called it. A typical valley cottage — diamond-paned windows, sweet pale green shutters, a giant sycamore shading the front lawn — it sat on almost an acre of land dotted with fruit trees. A perfect setting for dogs and babies. Alix had been right — they could never have afforded anything like it at the beach or even in town, especially after the renovations and converting the garage. The parklike setting was a haven after the steaming crunch of the freeway. Or would have been if Alix hadn't been perched on the edge of the couch when Molly opened the door. The thick heat seemed like nothing compared to what she faced now.

"One-thirty," Alix said, standing and slinging her purse over her shoulder.

"There was a major accident — "

"I just wish you could once be on time," Alix snapped.

"Look, I'm here now and we can either be on our way or sit and fight about it."

Alix glared at her.

Molly glared back. "I've got to pee. Then we can leave."

When she came back into the room Alix remained perched on the same spot.

"What," Molly demanded.

Alix didn't look up. "This is supposed to be a happy occasion."

"So were all the others," Molly shot back.

Alix's head snapped up as if she'd been hit. Her eyes registered hurt, her voice anger. "I'll just go alone."

She was out the door before Molly could stop her.

"Fuck," Molly shouted into the empty room. She kicked the chair nearest her. "Shit."


The lack of routine Molly decried after Oregon had become its own sort of routine, their life perpetually in abeyance while the inseminations continued.

She and Alix were busy, productive, not happy so much as just there in the house, in their lives.

Alix no longer asked for company when she went for her inseminations. Sometimes she didn't even tell Molly until the last minute when she was ovulating (once, when Molly had been under a killer deadline for the opening of a show, not until after). Molly knew though, from the discarded prediction kits in the garbage. She never mentioned them because Alix never mentioned them.

In this suspended animation they trudged toward the holidays. Between concerts and recording sessions Alix was booked solid.

A few days before Christmas Molly walked in from her studio and was greeted by steamy heat from the shower and the smell of soap and Alix's perfume. She followed the aromas into the bedroom. Alix moved frantically between the bathroom and closet, half-dressed in slip and pantyhose and fumbling with her earrings as she stepped into her black heels.

"I'm late."

Molly wanted to be aroused by Alix's state of undress. On past occasions she had been. Hands running over silky slip and stockings, she'd press Alix's bare chest against her. After hasty wet kisses and eager fumbling, giggling because they didn't even have time to lie down, thrilled by the challenge, Alix would finally leave, almost late, cheeks still flushed. "Something to remember me by," Molly would call after her. But tonight — any night lately — Molly could note only her own lack of interest.

Alix hastily ran down some messages for Molly,

then shimmied into her black dress — "concert drag," she called it.

"Could you?" she asked, turning her back to Molly, who zipped the dress. "Thanks, hon. How do I look?" Alix didn't really give her a chance to answer, just threw on her coat, missed Molly's cheek with her goodbye kiss, and headed to the door. "I'll be late. See you in the morning."

Molly stood in the empty room, surrounded by Alix's scents and a flickering memory of desire.


Molly and Alix divided holidays between their families. This year Molly's father had announced he'd be in Miami for Chanukah and Christmas. Ben's four sisters had moved there years before, when their husbands were still alive.

"You're starting to go down there a lot," Molly said.

"Jerome wants me to see his place." Ben's brother, Jerome, had moved there just recently. Ben was the last holdout, still practicing medicine and still living in Manhattan. "And the girls are lonely without Rita." His second oldest sister had died there just months earlier.

"So your sisters are pretty sad, huh," Molly said.

"Well, Rita was only eighty-five."

Alix often teased Molly about the Rubins' longevity. "I don't care if you remarry after I'm gone," she'd say, "just wait a respectable time, okay."

"What makes you so sure you're going first?"

"Are you kidding? Look at your family — they've all survived their spouses."

"That's my father's side. What about my mother?" Claire Rubin was only forty-seven when she died.

Alix shook her head. "You're too much your father's daughter."

Molly listened while Ben said he was going to spend the holidays in Miami. That meant Molly and Alix would go to Oregon — another stretch with the Chases, more Baby.

"At least we'll see each other in March," Ben said. His sisters had planned a big seventy-fifth birthday bash for him in Miami. "You're coming, right?"

"We wouldn't miss it."

So this year Christmas would be with Alix's family.

They arrived at the Chases just in time to balance their presents on the massive pile that threatened to topple the tree in Alix's parents' living room. They spent Christmas day in familial bliss with the Chases, watching Betsy smile at everyone and dribble food down her bibbed front.

"That was torture," Alix confessed that night in bed, shedding bitter tears, ashamed of her jealousy toward her brother and his wife.

Molly made appropriate soothing noises, but in reality she had gone numb.

They came home on New Year's Day because Alix had a concert. Molly picked up where she'd left off before the trip. Once she got into the groove of work she found it easy enough to settle back in to what now passed as their routine. Their only reality had become technology and tests and the monthly cycles of ovulation, expectation, and disappointment. Alix went to her sessions and to the doctor's. Molly scraped and mended and patched and matched colors. She had never felt so lonely.

One bright March morning Molly was working the daily crossword when a sleepy Alix stumbled into the kitchen, mumbling a greeting as she put up water to boil.

"Your coffee smells so good," she said as she opened a cabinet to select from an assortment of teas. "I'm so sick of this herb shit." She no longer allowed herself even decaffeinated coffee, even on weekends. She had vowed to keep her body as pure as possible until she got pregnant and then right through nursing. "How did you sleep?"

"Fine," Molly lied. She'd had the Dream of Ten Babies again. It had been part of her sleep pattern ever since the doctor's casual comment when she put Alix on her first dose of fertility drugs almost a year ago. "With Clomid, you don't get ten babies, that kind of thing," Susan Gates had tossed out.

As soon as Molly's head had hit the pillow that night she was in the delivery room and Alix was grunting and then laughing, gleeful, overjoyed, as her baby came neatly out of her. Susan handed it to Molly.

But then Alix giggled. "I think there's another."

Susan reached in and sure enough, soon they were popping out like nobody's business, and everyone was in on catching them — Susan and Norma and all the nurses and nurse practitioners. Molly had to hold them all, because Alix was too busy giving birth.

Molly wanted to laugh, and would have, if the dream had stopped there.

One last baby emerged, more real than the others, who all seemed somehow older, not really newborns, all capable somehow. But this one, this last one, was real, so real, and he came out looking for her, needing her. And Molly's hands had been too full to take him.

A deep cry — hers or the baby's, she wasn't sure — stuck in her throat and woke her. Alix rustled next to her, murmured, "I'm here, don't worry, go back to sleep."

But Molly had lain in the dark, heart pounding, afraid to close her eyes, afraid of that tiny needy face, and of that thick stifled moan. Death had been such a presence in her life ever since the first insemination. In addition to the constant thoughts about Michael and her mother, gloomy images of freeway accidents or devastating earthquakes and worse — violent shootings, mad scenarios — filled her mind when she was supposed to be working.

"Earth to Molly. Where are you?" Alix bounced her tea bag.

"What should I get my father for his birthday?" That's how it had gone the last few months. They talked across each other, around each other. If a question touched on a sensitive subject, simply avoid answering it.

Alix took the cues as easily as Molly. "I thought you decided on a cashmere sweater."

"Only because I'm totally uninspired and it's easy to pack."

Alix dumped the teabag. "How about a CD player?"

Molly thought for a moment. "That's a great idea. That and a few CDs."

"We can shop after my squirt if you'll come with me." Alix tried to sound casual.

Molly had come to regard Alix's inseminations as something Alix did regularly, on her own, like getting her hair cut or her teeth cleaned. "Why all of a sudden?" Molly asked.

"I've been asking for three years. That's hardly all of a sudden."

"You know what I mean." Molly hadn't gone since that crack she'd made months earlier.

Alix sipped her tea before answering. "Because this is going to be the last one."

"I've heard that before."

"This time I mean it."

Molly felt relief mixed with disbelief. She'd heard this before, too. "What about when Susan comes up with one of her tricks?"

"No more tricks, Moll. I've reached my limit." That's when Alix's tears started. She looked up at Molly. "It's never going to happen, is it?" Her hands shook. Tea sloshed over the mug, peppermint scented the air.

"You don't know that."

"I wanted to contribute something . . ."

Molly had heard all this before. The children-and-art speech. She let Alix talk, watched her blue eyes fill with tears that flowed down her cheeks from an endless source. When Alix seemed to run out of steam, Molly quietly reminded her, "You have your music."

"That's nothing. It doesn't go beyond me." Alix looked at Molly. Her tears had stopped. She put her hand to her chest as if to contain some dreadful pain and heaved a great sigh. "This was going to be our creation. One of the most important things we could ever do together."

As much as Molly wanted this to be over, she was moved by Alix's pain. She stood next to Alix and gently rocked her. "Maybe #453 wasn't such a good choice after all," Molly said.

They had spent days studying the donor lists Norma had given them. Dizzying columns of facts: height and weight and coloring, ethnic origin, hobbies, blood types. One bank provided brief profiles of its donors. They had decided on one with Molly's coloring. "I want our baby to look like us," Alix had said as she circled their selection.

Molly had come to feel a certain fondness for #453. He appeared in her dreams, sometimes looking a little like her brother Michael. She imagined their baby would look like Michael — though a row of Alix's nephews and nieces popped into her head to remind her the chances of that were slim to none. Molly continued to rock Alix, stroke her cheek.

"What if it's me?" Alix sniffled. "What if I can't ever conceive?"

What the hell, Molly thought, she must be as tired of this as I am. And if it's the last one . . . "Don't worry, baby, I'll go with you today."


"Hey, gals, how you doin'?" Tracy, the receptionist, greeted Alix and Molly as they stepped across the reception area to the desk. "I'll tell Katie you're here." Katie was one of three nurse practitioners Alix saw in addition to her doctors, Norma and Susan. Alix had confessed to Molly that she was always glad when Katie did the inseminations — she thought Katie's being a lesbian brought her luck.

Molly and Alix sat in deep couches to wait. Molly knew by heart all the pamphlets on the rotating rack in one corner, both the English and Spanish versions — on breast cancer and pregnancy and menopause, osteoporosis — and had come equipped with a spiral book of *New York Times* Sunday crosswords. Her job was simply to lend moral support, act as a good luck charm. Alix impatiently flipped through the magazines on the table in front of her, pictures of babies cooing at her from every glossy page. This was so routine. They were completely blasé.

How different from the first time, when Molly had huddled nervously with Alix on this very couch, jumped up eagerly when the nurse called Alix's name. She paced the room waiting expectantly for the results of Alix's ultrasound. When they confirmed that Alix was ovulating, Molly had bounded into the examining room to take her place at Alix's head, had gripped her hand while Norma readied her instruments.

"Okay, here comes the speculum. A little cold." But this was Katie's voice now, not Norma's. Molly looked down. Katie was readying the canula containing the washed sperm. Alix closed her eyes.

Any slim threads of hope left from the first year had snapped several inseminations earlier. Molly no longer believed in signs either. Early on, she'd experienced a surge of faith, an optimism uncharacteristic for her. That too had been shattered. But oh, the wonder, those first few months.

She remembered the astonishment they'd both felt that first time, the profound implications of the whole process, of each action Norma took. As Norma announced each step — "I'm inserting the canula now" — Molly had marveled at the cloudy substance that could change their lives. She'd felt different at that moment, that same difference when she'd lost her virginity. Invisible but unalterable. She couldn't begin to imagine how different Alix must have felt. As if responding to her thoughts, Alix kissed Molly's hand. A perfect telepathic moment, their thoughts joining as one. Until Alix had sniffled and said, "When I think of all the times I used to get this for free..."

The tension, released with their laughter, shook out a few tears as well. Molly, inarticulate with joy at what they were starting, had covered Alix's face with kisses.

Today Molly was hardly present. She thought about the pileup of projects waiting for her at the studio. She was here as a courtesy to Alix, she felt like a traitor for being excited at the prospect of this being the last time they'd have to go through this. The ramifications had begun to sink in. She thought of the time they'd have in Miami, the freedom to be a little looser with money. Maybe they could slip away to Key West for a night or two. Alix's insistent grip tugged her back into the moment.

Alix asked about Katie's lover and their son. They chatted about local news, Alix's latest sessions. They hovered on this casual level, but Molly heard the tension in Alix's voice, felt her grip getting tense and sweaty.

"Alix, did Susan talk to you about in vitro fertilization?" Katie asked.

Molly held her breath waiting for Alix's answer. She wondered if Alix had lured her here under false pretenses. Susan Gates was the infertility specialist.

Would Alix want to try this last-ditch effort — to the tune of about ten thousand dollars — before giving up?

"She told us, but it's too expensive and the success rate isn't high enough."

So this really might be it.

"Almost done," Katie said, squeezing out the full batch of #453, chasing it with an air bubble to make sure it was used up. "All gone."

Alix looked at Molly. "Was it as good for you as it was for me?" Alix's wry dry humor had given way to these nervous jokes, stale post-coital humor masking her fear and concern. But her expression asked, Will it work this time?

Katie took Alix's hand just before she left the room and gave it a squeeze. "You take care now."

Alix mustered a brave smile. "Keep your fingers crossed," she said.

Katie pressed Molly's shoulder on her way out. "Make sure she stays put for a few minutes." None of the doctors or nurses really thought that made much difference, but like serving chicken soup to bad colds, they felt it couldn't hurt.

Molly brought Alix's hand to her lips. "I'm sorry I've been such a schmuck lately," she said.

"You're not the only one." Alix closed her eyes. "What if it doesn't work this time?"

Six months' worth of ice melted as Molly stroked Alix's hair. "Don't worry about that now." Molly ran her hand across Alix's flat stomach. "Just relax."

Alix's eyes filled as she held Molly's hand. She whispered, "I want it so much."

"I know, baby, I know." Molly kissed the tears

that spilled now, kissed the corner of Alix's mouth. Her own tears fell on Alix's face.

They went to a movie after the visit to the doctor's, partly to avoid rush hour traffic into the Valley, partly to be together without having to talk.

Molly stared blankly at the screen, unable to pay attention to the film. What if it had taken this time? Just her luck for Alix to get pregnant on the last try, just when Molly figured she might not have to disappear. All these months they hadn't had to focus on anything but the various procedures Alix had to endure. The process of getting pregnant had become a separate reality, and Molly had virtually lost sight of its ultimate goal.

Up on the screen, a beautiful woman kissed a beautiful man. Bet they won't have our problems, she thought. She fidgeted in her seat. Alix absently put out a hand to still her. Just like old times — always reaching for each other, often unconsciously, for reassurance, comfort, distraction, balance.

By the time the movie let out traffic had cleared and they drove home in silence. Molly's mood had begun to change. The thought of getting their old life back cheered her. She felt like celebrating.

Alix was rather quiet. Always a little tense after a procedure, wondering what was going on inside her body. Tonight, Molly knew, she had the extra pressure of knowing she'd had her last chance. I can help her forget, Molly thought.

When they got home they put on Ella Fitzgerald

singing Cole Porter and started fixing dinner, filling a pot with water for pasta and sautéing vegetables. Molly's mood must have been contagious because while they waited for the water to boil Alix grabbed her and they danced in the kitchen.

"It isn't fair," Molly said as Alix led her around the butcher-block island.

"What isn't?"

"My parents had this and I had Iron Butterfly singing 'In A Gadda Da Vida.'"

Alix spun them around once. "We'll teach our baby to dance."

"What if she's a klutz?"

"Impossible." Alix dismissed the suggestion. "With your grace . . ."

"It won't have my genes," Molly said.

"Sure it will," Alix countered. "They're in me by osmosis or love or something. Photosynthesis."

"Alix . . ."

"Don't get serious on me now, Moll. We're dancing. Enjoy."

The song was ending. Alix dipped Molly who, unprepared, held herself stiff and tight. "Moll, you're thinking again." Alix pulled her up and they danced in place until the next song started. Alix picked up the rhythm and navigated them through the doorway into the dining room. Now Alix's enthusiasm was catching. This was almost like it used to be, Molly thought. Somehow they were back where they belonged, close and in love and Molly was comfortable enough to let herself come back a little as they danced into the kitchen, past their small breakfast table.

"Okay," Alix said, positioning them, "let's try it again with a little trust."

This time Molly let herself go. She leaned back, felt Alix's thigh beneath her, Alix's strong arm under her back. She was safe and supported. Alix held her there a good five seconds before lifting her upright and continuing their dance.

"Much better," Alix said.

Dinner went as smoothly as their dance. They ate in the living room and watched CNN. They sat surrounded by the accumulated details of their years together: bookcases filled with novels, biographies, art monographs; pieces they'd picked up on their travels — a bowl from Provincetown, a print from Carmel, rocks from Taos. The dog stretched out at Alix's feet. This felt like real life to Molly, as romantic as any date they'd ever had, any special meal with candles and music. The mood carried to bed where they started to make love. Not a passionate clash, but a comfortable friendly joining.

Molly broke from a deep satisfying kiss to ask, "How many times do you think we've done this?"

"Who cares," Alix laughed.

"Just a rough estimate, come on, what do you think?" Molly said. "A thousand times?"

"I don't know." Alix tried to slide down between Molly's legs.

Molly held her. "A hundred thousand?"

What started as a joke became reminiscing as they recalled specific times together — one particularly magical night in San Francisco — or odd places, like the front seat of the car while they were parked on a side street off La Cienega. The quickest time, before a dinner party, guests expected any minute, Molly had pressed Alix against the bedroom wall, no time even to pull down their pants all the way.

They came up with an estimated grand total of 2,187. According to their calculations, the first year together they'd made love somewhere between 1,300 and 1,560 times.

"Call it fourteen-fifty," Alix said. Molly agreed.

The numbers tapered off radically after that. Over three hundred times their second year, it was down to twice a week by the third year, from there to once a week, down to once and sometimes only every other week by their seventh and eighth years. But then, those were Baby years.

"Come on, we do it more than that," Alix said.

"Not lately," Molly said, kissing Alix's neck. She nuzzled closer to Alix, started moving rhythmically against her.

"Do you think that's sort of average?"

Molly traced her fingers along Alix's chest.

"Or less than average? Oh, God, is this lesbian bed death?"

"Now who's thinking?" Molly asked. She took Alix's hand, guided it between her legs.

Fragrant air wafted through the room from lemon and orange trees blooming outside their window. Alix busied herself with Molly's body, touching and stroking, tonguing and kissing. Months of distance faded as Molly traded Alix touch for touch, stroke for stroke. She was amazed that after all this time she could still feel so intensely, still long so much to give herself to Alix. And then all thought was blasted out of her head as she rocked toward number 2,188.

Alix's coming was loud and brilliant, as satisfying to Molly as her own. *Good,* she thought, settling into sleep without fear of what she'd dream, *we're getting back on track.*

Saturday morning Molly worked on a 19th-century copy of a 17th-century Titian. The surface of the painting had been like a dried-up lake bed, parched and crackled. She had to be careful with her Q-tip not to lift off any paint. Sometimes she used a scalpel to gently work loose softened varnish from the impastos of thick white highlights. After an hour she'd cleaned almost eight square inches. The progress she made, though slow, revealed a wonderful passage in the painting — like music, lyrical and lush. Small glimpses of possibility opened to her, just like passages between her and Alex since the last insemination.

She turned the radio to a classic rock station. The Beach Boys' "Surfer Girl" rocketed her back to the summer her family had rented a house on Long Island. Whole afternoons she'd sit in the back seat of her mother's rented convertible while Michael practiced for his driver's test. They'd do endless loops in the deep gravel driveway. A steady five miles per hour around and around — Michael perfecting his broken-U-turns and Molly watching the sky. She'd accompany him also on road trips with their mother or father.

Claire was by far the easier of their parents for driving practice. She just sat back, perfectly relaxed, as if she really enjoyed driving with her son. Ben, on the other hand, kept up a running commentary — "Didn't you see that? Watch for that Buick. Okay, now prepare for the turn." Michael didn't need the warnings. He was a good driver who paid studious attention to everything going on around the car — not just at intersections, but in the middle of the block, especially on those warm lazy streets where kids played on the lawns and chased fly balls with no thought to cars.

Molly remembered a touch football game they all played on the front lawn that summer. It had started spontaneously. Just back from a day at the beach, Molly and Michael had been tossing a frisbee. All day, no interpretation of the motto in raised plastic inside the disk — *Flat Flip Flies Straight* — helped her in the least. But now she finally had the hang of it and could make it sail the way Michael did.

Ben stepped onto the porch, a towel wrapped around his waist, wet suit in hand.

"Daddy, watch this." Molly sailed the frisbee to her brother.

"Dad, here." Michael sailed it to Ben, who dropped his suit to make the catch.

Their father motioned toward the far end of the lawn. "Go wide."

Michael started to run, dodging invisible tacklers in his path. As soon as he caught the frisbee, he sailed it back for Ben, already in motion on the grass. Ben then threw it to Molly, who relayed it to Michael.

"Okay, team." Claire stood on the porch now. "If you want hamburgers you've got to let your father start the coals."

Michael tossed the frisbee to her. She barely got "Mike —" out of her mouth before it reached her. She clapped down on it with both hands to cheers from her family.

Somehow Michael got them into teams then, him and Claire against Ben and Molly, everyone laughing and eager. Neither Claire nor Molly had any notion of the rules, but they had strategies. Molly ran full out to wherever Ben told her in the huddle. Claire was craftier. In the excitement of one play she lunged for Ben's towel. Clutching the terry cloth with one hand he tossed the frisbee to Molly who ran for her first touchdown.

Panting, she looked back from under the maroon leaves of the Japanese maple that served as the goal line. Long late afternoon shadows crept toward the bright spot where her family laughed, golden in the still-warm sun. Ben and Claire doubled over, intimate even in this public moment, Claire wiping her tears with Ben's towel. Michael, too, stood laughing and clapping, cheering for Claire's effort and Molly's score.

They had played for another idyllic hour or so, ending the game only when they could no longer see.

Molly's memory wasn't of the game so much as of the mood of the game, a golden moment replayed in slow motion, a nostalgic time before any tragedy or illness, the magic hour not truly representative of their life together but one she would never forget. She wished she could freeze them just that way, one happy family playing endlessly.

The songs from that summer — "Little Deuce Coupe," "Heat Wave," "One Fine Day," a bunch of Peter, Paul and Mary ballads — still made Molly feel safe. At least until the present intruded in the voice of the deejay. Molly's good mood fell, ambushed by other memories of the past. Although resigned to how things were she sometimes longed to have everyone back. She wished again for amnesia.

Molly swatted the off button just as the opening of "Leopard-Skin Pill-Box Hat" hit her ears. The first time she heard Bob Dylan had been through the door of Michael's bedroom. "Subterranean Homesick Blues." At first she'd hated the nasal twang, but Michael said Dylan was really good.

She remembered exactly what Michael wore that day — or maybe not that day exactly, but certainly often enough to make it more than likely he'd had on chinos and a white button-down shirt, white socks and penny loafers. Well, the penny loafers would be kicked off somewhere around the door to his room, lying haphazardly about until their mother told him to either put them on or tidy up. His room was filled with sporting equipment and weights. The decor was wood and plaid. What Molly remembered about her brother was his size and his solidity. He could tinker with models, delicate miniatures that cluttered his shelves and desktop. Or he could twist open the most stubborn jar lids for their mother.

Molly was only eleven when he died in a car accident that first summer he got his license. Typical B-movie story — great kid gets license and bad kid gets drunk and runs him off the road and around a tree. All she had now were the vaguest impressions of him — a sense of security when she'd been with him, and of protection — like slipping her hand into his at the airport on that trip to Bermuda. He'd seemed so capable, able to do anything. Anything except survive.

Molly's parents had tried to protect her from Michael's death, tried to return to normal as soon as possible after the funeral. They gave up the summer rental early and had returned to the humid deserted city. The apartment felt empty as well, as if only Michael's presence could make it complete.

Ben went back to work full time. Claire took Molly to the movies during the day to escape the heat and humidity. They saw *It's a Mad Mad Mad Mad World* and something with Doris Day and Rock Hudson, and at a revival house, *Little Women*. Molly remembered those afternoons, she and her mother in the dark, hands dipping into popcorn or boxes of Milk Duds or Nonpareils or Raisinettes. Claire cried throughout the films, without regard to what was happening on screen, tears streaming down her cheeks. They walked home afterward, sometimes buying a Good Humor on the street. Molly held her mother's hand, just as sticky and sweaty as her own.

When school started, Molly's teachers muttered condolences. Molly told a few of her friends, but none of them had much to say about it because, she realized later, they hadn't experienced death yet, except for grandparents, and that seemed a much more remote experience.

At home they pretended to avoid Michael's room, where everything remained intact for months after his death. Molly spent time there every day after school. She would tiptoe in to sit on his bed or at his desk. His presence was still very much there; the room smelled the same. Molly surprised herself by staying out of his hidden treasures, boxes and drawers he'd declared off-limits to her. By pretending to obey him, she kept alive the possibility that he would return.

One day she walked in and sensed a subtle difference — a lingering of her mother's perfume. Another time she noticed a faint impression on the usually taut bedspread and her father's aftershave hung in the air. Her parents didn't mention these private visits to the shrine. Soon other scents intruded — glass cleaner and furniture wax. And more of Claire and of Ben and of Molly, without any renewing visits by Michael, until Molly confused the smell of the room with Michael's smell.

Some months after Michael's funeral Molly sat at the dining room table with her notebook. Rarely was she allowed to do this, but her father was working there — stacks of medical files in front of him, catching up on paperwork — and Molly took advantage and brought her French homework. She worked very quietly. It was way past her bedtime and she didn't want to alert her parents to the hour. This evening, however, Claire and Ben seemed particularly distracted. They had talked in their room for a long time after dinner, their voices muffled through the door. Only once could Molly understand something Ben said: "I am not yelling." After some time only Ben emerged, followed by a gravid, unnatural silence.

As Ben filled in patients' histories and Molly described *le ciel,* which was *bleu,* and *les feuilles,* which were *vertes,* she knew this was about Michael. All silences were about Michael.

Claire came out of the bedroom and announced she was going for a walk.

"What do you mean?" Ben asked.

"You heard me." Claire took her coat out of the closet.

Ben looked at her but didn't get up. "You can't go out. It's too late."

Molly knew that these simple straightforward sentences her parents spoke held hidden meaning, another text entirely. But she couldn't translate them the way she could her French. She wouldn't understand until much later the anguish behind Ben's inability to dissuade his wife as she put on her coat.

"Where are you going to go at this hour?"

"Around the block or something."

Molly didn't know exactly what was going on, but she knew two things: her mother had never done anything like this before and her father clearly didn't want her to do it then.

"Claire, be reasonable." Molly could tell that he was trying to keep his voice normal. "I said you could get started on it. Just not yet."

"I've been reasonable for six months, now it's your turn. I won't live like this any longer." Claire walked over and kissed the top of Molly's head. "You go to bed soon." Then she left.

Ben worked in silence. Molly feigned interest in *les arbres* and *l'herbe* and *les belles fleurs* and waited for Ben to say something.

"Your mother . . ." Ben started, but then just slipped a completed file onto the stack to his left.

What had he been about to tell her? A story? The truth?

A couple of months after that Michael's room was redecorated, converted into a den no one used, a spare guest room no one ever slept in. With no site for Molly's small pilgrimages, her shrines to Michael became private, portable, carried inside her heart. For Ben and Claire he became photos on a shelf, promise denied, a silence.

Molly knew she couldn't go back to that moment at the dining room table and change the course of the evening, thereby altering the course of her life. What would she have substituted in its place? A town meeting for the survivors, an open forum where everything was discussed — the tragedy, the rage, the self-pity brought on by the death — anything but what turned out to be her key lesson in the art of subterfuge. It was another incident to forget, though its very nature made it one of those that clung to all her senses. She could still feel the pen in her hand, smell the smooth acid paper of her textbook. She heard the rustle of her father's papers, his constant muttering as he talked himself through each form, each case history. The dishwasher thrashed in the background. Her mother had made brisket for dinner, and the heavy scent of onions and meat overpowered the scene.

That night, Molly learned not to discuss it — because after all, the changes happened eventually. Michael's room disappeared as effectively as had Michael himself.

Of course nothing ever really disappeared. And even though Molly came to call herself an only child Michael lay deep in her experience. Or he had until three years ago.

For Molly dreamed practically every night of Michael. The dreams had started sometime in the first year of inseminations, accompanied by a sense of her mother's presence, just a fleeting glimpse of her face each night when Molly closed her eyes. Haunting dreams she couldn't remember tagged after her throughout the day, making a final appearance just as she was getting into bed again.

Maybe if the inseminations stopped the dreams would too.


Ten days after the insemination Alix still hadn't gotten her period. Molly's dreams and doubts intensified each day Alix didn't bleed. She tried to concentrate on work, tying up loose ends before leaving for Miami. She wrapped the CDs she'd bought her father.

Her parents hadn't been big on exchanging presents. They'd take each other out for dinner, or maybe a show. Buying presents for Ben became a challenge for Molly after Claire died. Year after year she went out of her way to outdo the last gift. An exercise bicycle, a year's membership in a health club, a night on the town for two, complete with limo. Gifts that kept giving — fruit and steaks delivered monthly, theater subscriptions. The unspoken requirement, self-imposed, was that they be grand enough or innovative enough or enough of a conversation piece to compensate for what Molly could never give Ben: the people he had lost.

Molly waited in limbo as, day after day, Alix put off the at-home pregnancy test. She knew Alix did this partly out of superstition — she didn't want to jinx anything — partly because she enjoyed the anticipation.

The day before they were to leave for Miami Alix burst into Molly's studio. "Let's go to the beach," Alix said. All her words these days rang with hope and excitement. Late periods were the biggest letdown for Alix, and Molly watched this time as she hung on the chance that maybe, just maybe.

"I've got to finish this." Molly was still working on the copy of the Titian. Only one tiny corner left to clean.

"Come on, the break will do you good."

Molly agreed to go because she saw something of the old pre-insemination Alix in her face, heard it in the lift in her voice.

"What a glorious day," Molly said as they spread out their towels. The waves came in clean recognizable sets, big and blue until they crested sea-foam green. Not a cloud in sight.

The few other beachgoers had scattered along the wide expanse of sand. The air smelled of salt water and tanning lotions, cocoa butter and lanolin. A couple played paddleball near the tide line.

They watched the water for a while, ate some fruit and cheese. Molly read until her eyes closed. In her dreamy state the waves sounded like thunder. A screech of gulls woke her. She looked up to see Alix putting on her sunglasses.

"Want to walk?"

They headed toward a rocky cliff at one end of the beach, climbed a sandy path that led down to a protected cove.

They stayed along the wet sand close to the water. Molly observed everything in sharpest focus, as if a veil had been lifted — no more gloom. The tide was out, and the pools were quietly active. At first glance the rocks rising out of the water appeared to be covered with moss and sand. On closer look they were alive with sea anemones seeming to have grown out of them. Each creature was a bright intricate object, a mosaic studded with bits of shell, seaweed, and sand. Molly uneasily touched one. It squirted a spray of water and squirmed shut.

Starfish littered the shallow pools. Despite Molly's "Don't," Alix wrenched a purple one from its nest and held it out for her to touch. It was stiff and rigid. Alix put it back where she'd found it, nestled against an orange one.

Alix stopped every so often to point out a crab or sea urchin, another starfish.

Molly wanted to thank Alix for dragging her to the beach. She brushed a lock of hair off Alix's forehead, put her arm around Alix's waist. Gestures and emotions came flooding back to her — how to behave on a romantic outing, the freedom of being in love. Tomorrow they'd go to Miami. No matter that they'd be spending time with family, the excitement of travel would bring them together. Molly counted on it.

"I wish I could hear something from one of these shells," Alix said.

"Like what?"

"Like, 'Forget it, you're not pregnant.' Or, 'Relax, it's a boy.'"

Molly kept her eyes down, not wanting to miss anything. She marveled at the rich life in the water. The ebb tide made deltas in the wet sand. Some rocks were studded with mussels.

She stooped to pick up an abalone shell. It was marvelous. Nacreous on the inside, its smooth shiny lip was iridescent, a sea-world of colors suspended in mother-of-pearl. Its drab outside would be a great shade for fabric: orange-browns with a subtle turquoise running in it. A row of holes pierced the edge, a recurring pattern she'd noticed in the other abalone shells strewn along the tide line.

"Moll, where are you?" Alix had stopped walking, and Molly crashed into her.

Molly held the shell up for Alix's inspection. "Isn't this beautiful?"

"Gorgeous." Alix dismissed the find. "Did you hear anything I was saying?"

"You wish the shells could talk."

"After that."

"I guess not."

"I said I want a baby."

Molly started to say she knew but Alix held up one finger to signal her to wait.

"Ever since the insemination things have been great between us," Alix said.

Yes, Molly cheered silently, she's felt it too.

"But I'm just not sure how you feel anymore."

"I feel like you do." Lame evasion, but the best Molly could come up with.

"And how is that?"

"Well . . ." Molly's heart raced, a nervous beat she felt in her stomach. What was this, fight or flight? "I guess excited. And scared. And I wonder . . ."

"What?"

"I wonder if you're not pregnant if we can go back to our real life."

"And what have the last three years been?" Alix squinted against the glare, hands on her hips, a mile of deserted beach behind her.

"I don't know." Molly's face grew hot. Her ears shut down. She'd stepped off the high dive and there was no turning back. "I feel like it was your idea."

"What, I roped you into this?"

"That's not what I said."

"It's what you think."

"I didn't say it."

"Molly, you know what these last three years have been for me? Hell. Sheer hell. Oh, fine at first, fun, exciting, whatever. But then wondering what was wrong with me because I can't seem to do this."

"There's nothing wrong with you," Molly interjected by rote.

Alix ignored her. "You weren't even there for the

last half of it. Three-quarters. Is that the kind of parent you're going to be?"

"Alix, calm down. I didn't say you roped me into anything." Molly fingered the shell in her hand, stared into it.

Alix snatched it from her and flung it into the ocean. "Pay attention."

Molly looked up. Alix's cheeks had the same red flush she got after sex. But unlike those times, Alix's eyes were sharp and dry, not full and open to her.

"I don't know what you want anymore, but this *is* my real life."

"We can figure all this out after Miami."

"I don't have anything to figure out."

Molly said nothing on the walk back. She flopped onto the towel, lay with her arm across her face.

Clouds covered the sun and the wind had picked up. Molly put on a sweatshirt. Everything had changed since the morning. The water was not blue now but dark gray, or maybe just a dark absence of color. The waves no longer came in clean sets but in short chops. Farther down the beach, near the cliff, they crashed in a confusion of foam, a tumble of incoherent poundings.


The next morning dawned foggy and cool. To avoid freeway traffic they took the coast route. The car moved through gray-white mists. Molly and Alix didn't speak, had barely spoken since they left the beach. The tenuous thread holding their peace together had snapped. Not even Molly's considerable mending skills could reassemble it. They'd eaten in silence, packed in silence. Alix had loaded the car in silence while Molly wrote a note for the friend who'd be taking care of the dog while they were gone.

They found a parking space and lugged their bags to the stop to wait for the bus to take them to the shuttle into the airport. They waited in silence.

Out of nowhere, Alix tugged at Molly's sleeve, inched her hand into Molly's, then grabbed Molly and held her very close.

"I love you so much," Alix said, lips against Molly's ear.

Instantly Molly's eyes filled. "You know I love you?"

Alix clung to her, nodded yes.

Molly started to step back, but Alix clasped her tighter. "I got my period this morning." The words came out in a muffled sob.

"Oh, baby," Molly said, rocking Alix gently.

"What am I going to do?" Alix wailed.

"You'll be fine, baby. We'll be fine." Molly absorbed as much of Alix's pain as she could, supported her lover who sagged under the weight of her grief. She stroked Alix's hair, swayed and comforted her until she stopped crying.


This changes everything, Molly thought as they boarded the plane. She thought of the last three years — the tests and the inseminations and the bills. The worrying and the waiting. The strain on their relationship. All for nothing, she thought. It would take time, but they'd be back in love again, just like before. She'd just have to be very careful with Alix, nurture her back to life.

She settled into her seat, fastened her belt. Alix absently thumbed through *Vanity Fair.* Molly had brought along a mystery but at the last minute had picked up a book of crosswords at the airport store. Now she got out her pen and the puzzles. She was well into the rhythm of the first crossword when they took off and had worked through several by lunchtime. The flight was uneventful, and Molly content for the first time in months.

She didn't know how to do Baby, but she could take care of Alix, no problem.

# FLORIDA

# *Molly*

Neither Ben nor Jerome was at the gate, so Molly guided Alix to the baggage claim area. They had barely spoken ten sentences during the flight. Not out of anger this time. Alix, too sad to speak, laid her head on Molly's shoulder. Molly raised the armrest between them and kept a reassuring hand on Alix's thigh. They had crossed the country in a sad togetherness, the closest Molly had felt to Alix in a long time.

They got their suitcases off the carousel, and were making their way to the exit when she heard Jerome calling them. "Hey, Molly! Alix! Over here!"

Her uncle moved quickly through the crowd. His old uniform — tweed jackets, vests, and bowties — a thing of the past, here he was tanned and casually dressed in a white warmup suit and Nike running shoes, one of those funny tennis hats perched jauntily on his head. A remarkably quick transformation, Molly thought, since he'd only recently moved to Miami.

Jerome didn't offer to carry their bags, merely grabbed them and headed toward the door. Already Molly could feel the Florida humidity, the heavy mugginess.

"We can carry those, Jerome, they're heavy."

"I'm retired, not dead." He set the bags down so the security guard could check the tags. "Ben's waiting in the car — all I needed was to let him get lost trying to find you." Ben had a dramatically bad sense of direction. "He's right out front."

Molly couldn't remember a time her father had been waiting for her at the gate. At the curb usually, or just pulling up. But never on time. If she closed her eyes and thought of her father she pictured him walking into a restaurant — or bar mitzvah or theater or airport, graduation, school event, whatever — scanning the room to find her and her mother. He always stood with his hands clasped in front of him, taking a moment to orient himself, his face showing no emotion, until the briefest smile indicated he had spotted them.

Jerome set her suitcase down near the curb. "Where'd he go? He was supposed to wait right here."

A foghorn hooted through the air. "That's him," Molly said, turning in the direction of the noise just as it sounded again. Ben had a stock of whistles: a sharp blast that would attract any cab within a ten-block radius, a warble, a foghorn, and a melodic lilt for which he needed both hands.

Molly stooped to pick up her shoulder bag. She tried unsuccessfully to wrestle a suitcase away from her uncle. She and Alix slowed their gait to his as they walked down the line of cars double-parked at the curb. Her father stood at the open door of a silver Thunderbird.

Each time Molly saw Ben she was surprised at how little he had changed. He seemed to age not annually but in plateaus. Stay the same for years, and then, suddenly, the next visit, he'd seem a little older, a little grayer, his posture a little more stooped. He looked no different today than he had six months earlier — perhaps a little better, dressed in a blue warmup suit and without the New York pallor even though he'd been in Florida only two days. Ever since Molly could remember, her father had spent his first day in the sun with an embarrassing amount of tanning lotion on his face, smeared over his bald spot, never quite rubbed in all the way. He'd start to look red before the afternoon, but that night at dinner, showered and shaved and cologned, he would look rested and tan, as if he'd been gone a week longer than the rest of them.

Jerome hoisted Molly's suitcase into the trunk and asked his brother, "Where'd you go?"

Ben gave Molly a quick light embrace. "You look good," he said. "You too." He hugged Alix. To Jerome, "They made me move."

"You should've told them we were on our way out," Jerome said, dropping Alix's carry-on into the trunk.

"I didn't know whether or not you were."

"Look at all those cars double-parked."

"They wouldn't let me do it. Jerome, that's upside

down." Ben removed the carry-on and flipped it over, tugging it so it rested lengthwise in the trunk, then changed his mind and switched it around again. He put Molly's carry-on atop Alix's, then next to it, asked for Alix's leather backpack to fit that in as well, played with that, too.

Jerome muttered "Such a fuss for a twenty-minute car ride."

"It took us an hour to get here," Ben said, satisfied at last.

"I wanted to try a shortcut." He shut the trunk.

"Some shortcut."

"I only made one wrong turn."

"And look where it got us."

"Fellas," Molly interrupted, "it's so good to be in Miami."

"Come on," Jerome said. "Pearl's expecting us."

Jerome drove. The brothers bickered about the best route out of the airport and occasionally tossed questions to Molly and Alix about the flight, what was the movie, how was the food. Molly jumped to answer, giving Alix every chance to remain silent, to stay out of the world until she was ready to come back.

Once over the Julia Tuttle Causeway they turned left onto Collins Avenue, the street that ran the length of Miami Beach. Hotel after hotel, big and little crammed together. Miami Beach seemed a caricature of itself, souvenir shops and hotels named to remind snowbirds from cold winters what they had come for — the Ocean Blue, the Ocean Grande, Ocean Haven, Ocean Horizon, Ocean Pavilion, Ocean Roc, Ocean Spray, Ocean Way.

Jerome's apartment, on the fourteenth floor of a

high-rise on Collins Avenue in Bal Harbour, had a terrace that faced another high-rise. If Molly turned to the right and leaned out she could glimpse the beach. White sand sloped into clear aqua which became deeper turquoise then sea blue-green. Clear and brilliant, the water here was an edible color. Tropical palms leaned in the wind.

Jerome hadn't brought any of his furniture from New York to this new place. With the help of a decorator he'd gone tropical, no signs of his former life among the rattan-framed couch and chairs, the glass-topped coffee table.

Framed pictures sat prominently displayed atop a rolling bar. "Are these the latest?" Alix asked, studying a group portrait of Jerome's daughter Leslie and son Aaron with their children.

"Three months ago. Alix, you should hear Andrea play the violin."

"Good?"

"Let's just say it's music only to a grandfather's ear."

Jerome led Molly and Alix to the guest room. This was where he had stashed his past, on the dresser and the walls. Wedding portrait — Jerome and Helen, so young and bright. Jerome in the army, with a snapshot of Jerome and Ben, both in uniform, tucked into one corner of the frame. Leslie as a baby, a toddler, in high school, on her honeymoon, pregnant, with the twins. Aaron and his wife with their children. The room was also a monument to Jerome's years in advertising. Posters of campaigns he'd written, pictures of him on location shoots, awards and citations he'd won. The room fairly burst with the weight of the past.

"Your father's going to move in with me while you're here. We'll see how long that lasts." He checked his watch. "You can freshen up or whatever, but don't take too long. Pearl's expecting us any minute."

As soon as he was gone Molly opened a window to let in some air. "How you doing?" she asked Alix.

"Fine."

Molly knew better than to push. Alix listlessly unzipped her bag. She looked tired. Her hair for once looked the "mousy" brown she called it over Molly's protestations. "No, just light brown," Molly would say, dipping her hand into the fine waves, wrapping it around her fingers.

Molly moved to her now, brushed a strand of hair out of Alix's eyes. She kissed Alix's cheek. "Come on, let's just keep moving, okay?"

They washed up and changed out of their airplane clothes. She gave herself and Alix a quick once-over in the mirror before stepping out into the living room.

Ben sat on the couch watching an old movie, eating a sandwich. He had changed into tan cotton pants and a pink knit cotton sweater Molly had given him. His white hair was wavy at the back and sides, top still combed — Molly knew by heart the elaborate ritual of slick back and notch forward with free hand — though these days there was not much left to comb.

He sipped from a glass of beer, wiped his lips with a paper towel.

"Dad, I thought we were going to Pearl's for dinner?"

"We didn't have lunch," Ben said. "Jerome, look at what's-his-name, how young he is!"

Jerome came out from the kitchen to look. He had changed, too, into white slacks and a navy shirt. "Jesus," he agreed with Ben. "Boy, he had hair then. I saw him on 57th Street last year. He's completely bald."

Molly sat on the edge of a chair.

"Don't get too comfortable," Jerome said. "Come on, Ben, the girls are waiting."


The doorman nodded to them as they stepped into Pearl's lobby. Molly took a few deep breaths as she waited for the elevator with Ben and Jerome and Alix.

The aunts had lived in Miami for a long time, since Molly was in grade school. They'd all left New York with their husbands, lived in houses while the children grew up and moved away. After their husbands died they sold their houses and moved into condos.

Of course they'd all come up for Michael's funeral. But Claire, never particularly close to her sisters-in-law, withdrew even further after that. She couldn't stand the sympathy or the hushed tones, the moment's hesitation before the other women boasted of the achievements of their sons, bragging curbed out of respect for Claire's loss.

They'd trekked up again for Claire's funeral. Molly had already met her first lover by that time, and turned to her for support and comfort. Still, at twenty she barely knew what to do for herself and had no idea what to do for Ben, and was relieved when the aunts descended. They came every night to sit shiva. They threw out all the medications left over from Claire's illness and put the apartment in order. They eased Ben back into his routine. Ruth interviewed housekeepers. By the time they left Ben's freezer overflowed with months' worth of dinners and he was working like a zombie, clutching at his practice to keep him afloat.

Except for a vacation or two and a few funerals, Molly hadn't seen her aunts often. Even though they lived apart, and each had her own personality, she always thought of them as a unit. The Girls came in a group. They filled a room with their presence. Lots of noise if not great physical volume. Molly pictured them as a bunch, a mass, couldn't separate them in her mind. And now this block of family loomed upstairs, all the more imposing to her because she knew they waited eagerly for tales of morning sickness and bassinet shopping.

No sooner had they stepped off the elevator than Zelda's thin wail pierced the dark hallway. "They're here!" And then Pearl yoo-hooed from the door to guide them as Ruth rushed past her sisters toward Molly, arms wide.

"Hello, hello, hello! Welcome to Miami! Let me see you. You look marvelous." Another big hug.

Crushed to her aunt's chest Molly marveled at the strength of this eighty-year-old. They bumped down the hall together, Ruth not willing to release Molly even when Zelda swooped down for her kiss. They had to separate to pass through the door into Pearl's apartment.

Pearl zipped out of the kitchen for the briefest of enthusiastic hellos before hustling back to tend to the main course.

Molly felt she had emerged from a time machine. Except for the tropical backdrop out the terrace window, she could have stepped across the threshold of Pearl's West End Avenue apartment. There were all the same smells and sounds from gatherings past, the dishes on the sideboard and the table set for fewer people but with the same baskets of bread and plates of butter and the nut dishes and the covered pots on the hot tray.

The sisters even looked the same, like Ben, no apparent aging. Pearl's skin was smooth and clear. Her hair had been red for so long that no one remembered its real color. Zelda had stayed a brunette for years, only recently adding frosted highlights. Only Ruth had let her short hair go gray.

No sooner were Molly and Alix kissed and made a big deal of than the Girls had other tasks to perform — put something into the oven, take out something else, set out the chopped liver. Questions for Molly and for Alix crossed the room, answers trailed after the aunts as they put final touches to the dinner.

"Jerome," Ruth called, "come open the wine. I asked at the store and they said this was good with turkey. Is it? I don't have anything else so I hope he was right."

"Alix," Pearl called, "come check my salad dressing."

Left alone in the living room, Ben and Molly sat for a moment like strangers, the first guests who happen to arrive at the same time and the hosts aren't dressed yet. Ben crunched a few nuts. Molly looked around the room. Mementos filled every available surface. Photo albums rose precariously high on end tables and bookcases. Elegant silver frames vied for space next to lucite cubes and plastic souvenir folders labeled "My Vacation" or "Brag Book." Grandchildren shoved against cousins who jostled relatives from the old country who welcomed the great-grandchildren crowded against them.

"How's my favorite niece?" Pearl referred to each of her nieces and nephews as her favorite. "How are you, darling?" Pearl's accent like a thirties movie — generic patrician but with a touch of Brooklyn thrown in. Pearl was eighty-five but no one ever guessed more than seventy-eight. Tonight, thrilled at having the family together, she seemed younger than ever. She grabbed Molly's chin in a freckled hand and planted a kiss on her cheek. "Ooh, I just love looking at you. Doesn't she look like me, Ruth? When I was her age?"

Pearl was always saying that and Molly, to her dismay, could see now that it was true, with the exception of hair color. Molly had always wanted to look like her mother. Instead she had inherited all the traits that characterized the Rubin women: large breasts, great legs, long faces, a tendency to gain weight through the torso.

A buzzer went off in the kitchen and Zelda called out, "Pearl, have you forgotten dinner?" Pearl and Ruth hurried away.

The pile of voices in the kitchen tumbled into the living room, Pearl's lifting above the others. "Here, put the turkey on this board. Zelda, here."

"I've got to have it here to carve it."

"You're not going to carve it."

"I always carve."

"Ben will carve it tonight. Ben! Ben! Come carve the turkey."

Ben didn't move. He put another handful of nuts in his mouth.

"Dad, they're calling you."

"They're not ready yet."

And from the kitchen, "Wait, it's got to set."

The old familiar argument. How could Molly have forgotten. Her uncles Sy and Larry had almost come to blows one Thanksgiving over this very issue.

Ruth bustled out of the kitchen and placed a platter of vegetables on the hot tray. "So tell me, Molly, how's everything? I can't wait to hear." No sooner said than she sped back for another load.

"It's always so peaceful here," Molly said to Ben, who smiled.

Finally everyone gathered at the table. Dishes were passed and wine was poured and everyone spoke at once. Molly again had that sense of time warp. This could have been any meal she'd had with the family since childhood. The Girls hurled a million questions at her and at Alix, about work and California and how they found Ben. "Great, right?" It went on. "So glad you're here." "What do you want to drink? Try this wine. California has good wine, don't you think, as good as French, they say." "Is that all you're eating?"

The hardest to handle were the questions about babies. "How's it coming, any results yet?" Pearl asked.

"If they had any news Molly would have told us," Ruth said. "Have you decided on a name yet?"

"Not really," Alix said.

"Of course." Ruth nodded. "You're not there yet."

"You know," Pearl said, "Claire really is a lovely name. So's Michelle. Maybe Claire Michelle. Or Mona, or Monica. Cathy's nice too."

"They could have a boy," Ruth said. "Michael. Or Carl. Mitchell. Malachi."

"Oh, please," said Pearl. "Malachi. The poor boy wouldn't be able to leave the house with a name like that."

"Don't forget Robin or Rachel or Robert," Zelda said.

Pearl explained to Alix the Jewish custom of naming a child after a dead relative. A watered-down version held that you could use the first letter of a name. The R Zelda suggested was for Rita, the oldest sister, who had died less than a year before.

"Both your parents are alive?" Pearl asked Alix, who nodded. "That must be so nice for you. And they must be so excited about this."

Molly tried to deflect the questions from Alix, tried to steer the conversation away from babies. "Alix might play on the next Barbra Steisand album."

Oohs and aahs and a launch into everyone's favorite singer: Sinatra vs. Torme, don't forget Ella Fitzgerald.

Her family took up so much space it seemed impossible that there would be room for one more person, one more voice added to the din, one more opinion tossed into the pot. And yet there had been more — Rita and Jack, Larry, Sy, Morey. Saul and Lucille. Helen. Claire and Michael.

In one sense, tonight was really no different. Everyone talked at once, gesturing and passing food and eating. When she left, her ears would ring the way they did after a rock concert or a loud bar — the deadness of tone after all that noise. Her family didn't simply take up space, she thought, they consumed it.

"I was watching Oprah and she had on people who'd had plastic surgery," Ruth said, one eye out for trouble. The only given at family gatherings was constant squabbling between Zelda and Pearl. "These were men and women — and not just nose jobs — I mean chins and cheeks — both kinds. You name it, they've had it changed. Can you believe people would do that to themselves?" Ruth's gaze jumped from Molly at the slightest rise in volume from the other end of the table, her attention divided like her loyalties. "I think —" But Ruth never finished her thought.

"It wasn't the A&P, Pearl," Zelda was saying at the other end of the table.

"Yes, it was. Momma sent Ben to the A&P —"

"We didn't have an A&P in the neighborhood. It was, I can't remember, but it wasn't the A&P."

"It was the A&P. Ruth, tell her it was the A&P."

"Zelda, does it matter whether or not it was the A&P?" Ruth turned to Pearl. "It was the market near the corner. Can't you just say it was the market near the corner?"

"Sure I can say that. I can say the A&P was the

103

market near the corner." Pearl sat back, challenging Zelda.

"So what was the story, Aunt Pearl?" Molly asked.

"Well, your grandmother sent your father to the A&P —"

"It was not the A&P," Zelda muttered loudly.

Pearl raised her voice a notch. "To buy prunes — Zelda, why do you always have to contradict me?"

"I'm not contradicting, I'm merely pointing out."

"So Grandma sent Daddy to buy prunes," Molly prompted.

"Right, and he came back without them. And Momma asked what happened and he said they didn't have any. And she said, I always buy them there, how could they not have any? And he said they didn't, that's all."

"But that wasn't the point," Zelda said.

"And what was the point of my story?" Pearl wanted to know.

"The point was that he asked the grocer for *flomen* and the grocer didn't understand him, that's the point. Ben didn't know the word for prunes in English."

Molly turned to Ben. "I thought you didn't speak Yiddish."

"We didn't. Momma and Poppa did. And who knew it was Yiddish — I'd never heard them called anything but *flomen*."

"See, I knew it was about *flomen*," Zelda gloated.

"I was getting to that part," Pearl said. "And it was the A&P." She folded her arms across her chest.

"That's enough," Ruth said. She began to sing, and again Molly remembered holiday dinners and special occasions, the grown-ups still at table, napkins amid the coffee cups and breadcrumbs. She and her cousins, playing in another room, would hear the songs and come back to sing along or just to watch.

Midway into a verse Ben joined in with a trilling lilt almost like birdsong.

Jerome had a request. "Ben, do that other one you do. The one with both fingers." Ben complied, pressing his index fingers against his tongue and blowing his most versatile whistle.

"Alix, this got us in trouble during the war," Jerome said. "Did Ben ever tell you?"

"We were both in uniform and were out with dates. We hit all the jazz clubs on 52nd Street. I think we ended up at Bill's Gay Nineties? Was that it, Ben? Or —" Jerome glanced at Zelda — "wherever, it doesn't matter. Anyway, we're pretty drunk by now because everyone's buying us drinks 'cause we're in uniform and it's wartime. So I try and get your father to whistle like that but he's too shy, of course, so I tell him to whistle and I'll pretend it's me. So he leans under the table and whistles and I stand up and put my fingers in my mouth like this. . ." He demonstrated for everyone, as Ben gave him a few bars of "It Had To Be You." "I'm having the time of my life but there's a band on stage and we're busting up their act, and next thing I know we're out on the street. Remember, Ben?"

Pearl said, "We could use you two in our act."

Molly thought this was a joke. "What act?"

"No one told you?" Ruth asked. "Ben, you didn't tell her about our act?"

"Ben, how could you not tell her?" Zelda grumbled.

Ruth started the explanation. "You know I always did volunteer work at the hospital in Bayside."

"Ruth, we all do volunteer work here," Zelda interrupted.

"But it was Ruth's idea," Pearl reminded everyone.

"It was not," Zelda protested. "I said we should get some songs together —"

"*Ruth* said we should get some songs together and perform for some of the seniors at the hospital." Pearl turned to Alix. "You know, show tunes and our kind of music."

"I remember very clearly," Zelda said. "We were having lunch . . ."

"Come on, Zelda," Ruth and Pearl chorused.

A sharp whistle silenced them.

"Thank you, Ben," said Ruth. "Anyway, we've got this little act and we take it to hospitals and convalescent homes and senior centers. Nothing big, but they enjoy it."

"We're getting quite a reputation," Pearl added. "Someone called from WTVJ. I can't believe your father didn't tell you."

Alix asked to hear one of their songs and the Girls launched into a *Fiddler on the Roof* medley. They were no more in key than they'd ever been, but for the first time everyone knew all the words, no more la-la-la-ing over rough spots — they were professionals now.

To much applause the sisters rose in unison and started to stack plates. Molly and Alix offered to help with the dishes but were shooed into the living room with Ben and Jerome, who turned on the television. "You like the Lakers, Alix?"

"They haven't been the same without Magic or Riley. But I don't follow basketball much. I like the Dodgers."

"What happened to them? Ever since they won the pennant in 'eighty-nine."

"They got rid of too many players when they should have gotten rid of Fred Claire."

This was just like being with Alix and her brothers. Molly didn't know what they were talking about. She'd only been in Miami for two and a half hours. She had three days left to go. She stepped onto the terrace for some air.

Glow from the high-rises lit the beach and obscured the stars. Surf pounded in the distance. Molly leaned against the railing, chin on her arms.

She'd been relieved when the singing started because it took the focus off her and Alix. They had diplomatically fielded all her aunts' questions about babies and pregnancy. The aunts had been so thrilled from the beginning — they'd make booties, blankets, "Bring the baby to Miami, we'll baby-sit" — she had never talked to them about ambivalence. Never explained the pressure she'd felt from what she called not Alix's biological clock but Alix's biological imperative.

The glass door slid open and shut behind her. A loud perfume reached her. Had to be Zelda.

"How can you stand it out here? Don't you hate the humidity? I never liked it, and now look at me, living in Miami. I wanted to move to the desert. That's the climate I like. But no, everyone had to come down here for Pearl. Look at my hair, it just wilts."

"I think it looks nice, Aunt Zelda."

"Really?" She patted it into place. "I've got a new fellow doing it." Zelda barely paused before patting Molly's arm. "You know, when Larry and I were first married we tried for the longest time. My friends were having babies right and left, like there was nothing to it. I wanted to have lots of kids — guess it's just what you're used to — but it was so hard we stopped after Sam. Who knows, maybe if we'd had more . . ."

Zelda's son Sam had always been trouble, a real discipline problem. He outgrew their excuse of "high spirits." They'd sent him to special schools, even to a psychiatrist. Eventually he'd run off to Montana with a girl he met in high school. "Who ever heard of Jews in Montana?" had been the family's general response. "He'll be back." But he never came back and he never kept in touch, not even when Larry had his heart attack and was dying. Zelda's unfinished thought — so often expressed over the years that it no longer needed completing — was that if they'd had another child she wouldn't be alone now.

"Anyway, sometimes even under the best of circumstances these things take time. You tell Alix I said that." Zelda pulled her blouse away from her body. "I hate this humidity. Two seconds and already I'm schvitzing. Come back inside."

Alix was the only one awake. Jerome dozed at the opposite corner of the couch, feet propped on the coffee table. Ben lay in Pearl's Barcalounger, hands on his chest, head back, an even snore whistling into the air. Her father was the only person Molly knew who fell asleep percussing his own chest. She had watched him perform this sort of self-hypnosis for years, one hand moving flat along the surface, the middle finger of the other striking rhythmically. Tap-tap to check the lungs — no dull areas, clear. Sharp raps down along the sternum, tap-tap-tap. Cardiac size good. Off the chest now to get the liver edge — tap — clear. Tap. Stomach A-okay. Tap-tap-tap-tap-tap back up to the collar. Tap . . . tap . . . tap. Getting sleepy now. Tap. Tap. Head dropping back, and he'd be out until Molly turned off the television, when of course his head would snap up. "I was watching that."

She studied his face. She suspected sleep was her father's means of escape, his only way to peace. Stress from work? Fall asleep after dinner. A boring party? Close your eyes. Too much pain because your wife and son are dead? Work harder, make another house call, go to sleep.

Who was Molly to argue? She had used her own ways of shutting herself off from Alix during the past year or so, fleeing to her studio early in the morning, sometimes going back in after dinner.

They used to escape together, leave town spur of the moment for a long weekend in Palm Springs or San Francisco, Carmel. They improvised their own holidays because Alix often had to work during what everyone else called the holiday season. One February they made a wind-swept drive all the way up Highway 1, past San Francisco, clear up to Mendocino, to a rented house on a bluff overlooking the rugged coastline. A foggy two days in and out of the hot tub, in and out of bed, getting rid of tension together, escaping together, never dreaming that one day they'd consider escaping from each other.

Nostalgia for times like that made Molly resolve to work toward just that again. That's how it had been, and that's how it will be soon, she thought. She tiptoed over to sit cross-legged on the floor at Alix's feet, pretending not to want to disturb Alix who had enveloped herself in the cable sports station as if she cared about it.

No sooner was she settled when Pearl's call came from the den. "Ben, Jerome, come look. Molly, Alix." The men stirred and opened their eyes. Ben reached out his arm for Molly to pull him up, and they marched down the hallway.

Ruth sat between Pearl and Zelda on a small sofa surrounded by what seemed like every photograph ever taken of the family. Pearl had albums and booklets and framed photographs. Weddings and bar mitzvahs and vacations and anniversaries. Occasions special and not.

Lots of stories about Poppa and Momma. Molly had never known her grandfather Max except from photographs. (Molly's name came from him. She hated the roundness of the word, its lack of grace, but preferred it to Maxine.) A dashing gent, he wore vests always and spats. But it was hard for her to picture her grandmother as the authoritative matriarch they called Momma. Grandma had been frail and tiny and ancient ever since Molly could remember. Nothing like her daughters were now.

Though Molly had heard these stories before, she could never keep track of the details — which great-uncle had opened the first store, which mustached and spatted dandy had courted her grandmother before Max came along and won her heart. Alix on the other hand remembered every face, every photograph, knew which scoundrel had opened a competing shop or stole dress designs. Soon the aunts were addressing their stories straight to Alix, accompanied by the usual arguments. The noise seemed to hone in on an ache starting just behind Molly's eyes. She marveled at this compulsive need to remember. Her attention strayed in and out of the conversations.

Pearl and Ben sat near her, studying a group of photos from Ben's high school graduation. Pearl rattled on about how good looking her brother had been, what fun they all had together in those days. How it was going to be like that again, with them all together.

Pearl poked Molly. "How do you like that about Dad being down here all the time? Isn't it great?"

Molly looked up but didn't say anything. Ben looked through the magnifying glass at a picture of his father.

Pearl looked at Ben. "You didn't tell her?" She turned to Molly. "Your father's moving down here full time. He's going to get rid of the apartment."

Molly tried to sound calm as she asked what Ben would do without his practice, without his housekeeper Jin. Had he even told her yet? But panic lurked underneath her words. Pearl and Ben spoke of Ben unloading the New York apartment as if it were a heavy burden he'd been carrying. But to Molly the apartment on 54th Street was home. No matter how long she lived in L.A., New York was home. And home was where she could always go, her last resort. No matter how long she was with Alix, deep inside she always envisioned herself on her own, ending up back in New York should she and Alix break up (not so strange a fantasy these past few months). She imagined herself living in a tiny apartment or even in her old room in her father's large apartment in some bizarre continuation of her childhood.

The rest of the evening skipped by Molly. She kept missing sentences, asking her aunts to repeat what they'd said. Easy enough to blame it on the rigors of travel.

Ruth told her brothers, "Take her home and let her get some sleep. They've had a long day."

She and Alix didn't talk as they got ready for bed. Under different circumstances, Molly would have turned to Alix for sympathy and encouragement. But Alix thought Ben's move was a great idea.

"You didn't think he'd work forever, did you?"

Well, as a matter of fact, she had. She couldn't see Ben's leaving New York as anything but a desertion and a betrayal. New York was Michael, her mother.

Molly saw that touch football game again. It played silently, a golden film flashback. She ached to crawl into the scene. She didn't know how to convey the sense of upheaval she felt, motherless and homeless, with an acute sense of loss past and future, no anchors or safe harbor.

Alix kissed her then curled away from her to go

to sleep. Too afraid of dreams, Molly pulled out her crossword puzzles. When she finally turned off the light the last thing she saw was the grid, its parallel rows and columns separating and drifting apart, herringboned at first, until they split and finally floated free, unencumbered by form.

# *Alix*

Ice. Ice cold. My mother's hands, source of
comfort, her warm and capable, no-nonsense,
always-there-for-you hands, quintessential mother's
hands, had become ice. The steamed vegetables
cooled in the dish the instant my mother picked it
up and handed it to me. The white walls ice blue,
no warm glow from the candles in the center of the
table. The flames burned straight and cold in the
still air. No conversation. Icy silence. No how was
your day, week, the last two months. That's how
long it had been since I'd seen my parents, since the
evening I'd come out to my mother.

That meal two months earlier had started off
soft, pink, the food spicy and bubbling. My mother's
lasagna set off conversation, elicited my compliments.
She deflected them: "Thank your father, I made it

because it's his favorite." Dad laughed and reminisced about their trip to Italy and then I chimed in with details about the recording session of Italian composers I was playing with the Hollywood Bowl Orchestra. Everything flowed into something else, warm and glowing, a happy family, safe, safe at home.

And I, newly safe and in love with Molly, was fairly bursting to tell them my happiness. I hadn't told them about any of the others because none had been so important to me. But I was going to move in with Molly, the first time I'd lived with a woman I loved. Aside from not wanting to worry about how to explain why this woman answered my phone, why I living with a woman, I wanted my parents to know this person who made me so happy. I thought they would be happy for me because I'd found the same thing they had — someone I truly loved, who truly loved me, someone to build a life with, raise a child with.

It was my last night in my own apartment, Molly's and my last night away from each other. Fortified by past experience — my family had always supported me in everything I did — I had arranged to have dinner with my parents.

After we ate, I helped my mother with the dishes. The kitchen was hot, steamy now from the lasagna pan soaking on the counter. My mother would get to those later. She started with the delicate coffee cups, washing each by hand. I dried.

My mother rattled on about Steve and Maddie, who were expecting their second child. Mom was thrilled, couldn't wait to be a grandmother again. "I always thought you and Jonathan would have such beautiful children." She sighed. "But I guess it wasn't meant to be. And you know I just want you to be happy. I'd hate for you to be alone."

I saw my opening and took it. "Well, as a matter of fact, Mom, I'm in love."

My mother squealed.

"It's a little different this time, Mom. I'm in love with a woman. Her name's Molly. I've never been happier."

I didn't give her a chance to interrupt, I poured out my love, praised Molly's character and achievements, bombarded my mother with all that was good and right about our relationship. Only then did I give her an opportunity to ask questions. A saucer slipped out of her hands. The shattered porcelain on the linoleum gave her an excuse to busy herself with cleaning up. She didn't look at me. She said she had no questions.

She took a dustpan and small brush out of the broom closet. As my mother daintily picked up the biggest pieces and put them on the counter, I told her a little more about Molly, how talented she was, how kind. My mother brushed the splinters and chips into the dustpan. I told her I'd never felt like this about anyone before. My mother wet a paper towel and knelt to wipe away the fine dust that remained. I offered to bring the broken pieces to Molly to see if she could fix them. I was trying to impress my mother.

"That's what she does for a living, but with really valuable art."

"Then she wouldn't bother with anything this cheap, would she." The ice had crept in already, but I didn't realize this at the time.

"I'm not saying it's cheap."

"Your grandmother gave me these dishes when I got married."

"I know."

"You can't buy better than Limoges."

"I didn't mean it's not good, just that it isn't antique."

"Then your friend wouldn't be interested in this, would she." My mother shook the wadded up paper towel in my face for a moment. Her own face masked her feelings, but her eyes were blue ice. She dumped the towel into the trash compactor. She gently gathered the bigger pieces, jagged shards that rattled in her trembling hand, and carefully laid them on top of the heap.

I went into the den. Before I could sit down my father shuffled a deck of cards, fanned them and held them out to me. "Pick one."

"Dad, my head is splitting."

"Humor me. I'm working on a new trick."

Suddenly my mother stood next to me. "Let her go, Tom."

"Night, Dad." I leaned to kiss him, my mother standing sentinel beside me.

She walked me to the door, something she only did for visitors. We kids came and went as if we still lived there. She grabbed me at the threshold. "Don't tell your father. It would kill him."

I drove straight to Molly's. She wasn't expecting me, and her face lit up when she opened the door. I saw my own distress reflected when her smile fell.

"I told them," I said. She didn't say anything, just reached out both arms and pulled me to her. She rocked and cradled me as I related what had

117

happened, tears hot on my face, burning against the chill left over from my mother. I cried as much from surprise as hurt and anger.

Molly undressed me. She put me to bed, turned out the lights in the apartment, then joined me. She offered to get me a T-shirt because I was shivering, asked if I wanted to take a hot bath, but I just wanted to feel her next to me. She got under the covers and I curled into her warmth and made her tell me again about her family, all her aunts and her uncle and how when Molly came out to her Aunt Ruth her aunt had said, "As long as you're happy, that's the most important thing." How her father had said, "I'm not surprised," then invited her and her lover to dinner that weekend.

The whole time she talked she stroked my back. Her hands were warm on my body.


My mother called the next day to tell me that what I was doing was wrong, disgusting, how could I do this to her, betray her like that. "You used to be normal. Can't you go back to being normal?"

I tried to explain, but nothing I said moved her in the direction of tolerance, much less acceptance, of what she called my choice.

"It's unnatural," she screamed into the phone.

"It's the most natural thing I've ever done," I yelled back.

Over the next few weeks I tried everything. I reasoned, explained, quoted studies and articles. No words penetrated her armor. No matter how I approached — calmly, cautiously, logically taking her through each stage in my development, each realization in my process — no matter how I argued that I was still the same person, or probably even a better person since I was being true to myself now, my mother's mind remained closed.

Of course she told my father. And my brothers.

Jack and I are closest in age. One day he stopped by to see my new place. Molly wasn't home but my friend Sharon was visiting with her ten-year-old daughter. After Sharon left, Jack leaned back on the couch, asked if I'd spoken to Mom lately.

"You know I haven't." I had little patience with his mission to make peace between me and my mother.

"Hey, she'll get over it," Jack assured me. "Just give her some time."

I thought he was right. I still trusted my family.

"I don't care what you do, as long as you're happy," Jack said.

I said thank you and meant it. My other brother had called to inform me I was no longer part of the family.

Jack changed the subject, asked how Sharon was doing. We chatted about her for a while. Jack slipped in a compliment about how well Sharon had raised her daughter. "Though if I were her I wouldn't have my child around you."

Blindsided. As soon as I caught my breath I asked him to leave. I told him I wouldn't be around him or anyone else unless they respected me and were nice to me. Jack said he didn't understand what he'd done to deserve that. I told him to think about it.

119

Since he was the only one who'd spoken to me, I didn't have any contact with my family after that afternoon. Molly talked me through my misery. Time was on my side; they'd come around. What if they don't? I'd ask. They would, I'd see. I was too close before for them to drop me forever, she'd say.

I had my doubts. Sometimes Molly admitted hers, too. Some families never come around.

What a strange period that was: miserable because I couldn't see or talk to my family, yet thrilled to be living with Molly, adjusting to our life together, learning each other's rhythms.

Five months after I came out to her my mother found a lump in her breast. I thought her illness would help her focus her priorities, see that my being a lesbian was not as important as how much I loved her, how much she loved me. But the crisis only served to enlarge that block of ice around her heart. My mother's cancer was my fault. I was blamed by my brothers, my father, my aunt, a cousin, and of course by my mother. She wouldn't let me come to the house to see her.

I found out only by accident that she had had surgery to remove the lump. I went to the hospital to see her. We hadn't spoken in three months.

She had a corner room. I arrived at noon and the July sun burned outside, overexposed the white sheets and the stainless steel paraphernalia in the room. It reflected off the patterned linoleum. I regretted not bringing a light sweater, since the hospital was maintained at a chill seventy degrees.

The rest of my family must have been at lunch. Pale and ice white, my mother lay against the sheets. I stood frozen by the foot of the bed wanting to reach for her hand, the one not encumbered by the IV.

Her eyes fluttered open. She almost smiled. I recognized her face for one split second. That's all it took for her memory to come back, to fill in the last five months, flesh out my betrayal. No more smile. Her face became a mask. "What are you doing here?"

"How did it go?" No one had told me the results of the tests.

"Get out."

"Mom."

Louder: "Get out."

I stood rooted in the glare of the useless sun.

She shouted at me. "Get out or I'll have you thrown out."

I stumbled blindly to the waiting room where Molly sat. She guided us to the elevators. I leaned on her all the way down. She placed a firm hand at my elbow when the doors opened. I walked smack into my father and brothers.

I didn't know what to do. Molly stood right by me, ready to follow whatever cue I gave. Steve wouldn't even look at her, but he shot me a dark glare before stepping around me to the control panel. Jack followed Steve. But he nodded at me and, by extension, Molly.

My father just looked at me. His eyes, bluest movie-star eyes, seemed so sad. (My father and my brothers all so lost and sad without my mother, even without me, for we're the strong ones, my mother and I. The men in my family are just mass and muscle waiting for direction.) My father opened his arms to me and I stepped into their circle. How thick he seemed after Molly; my arms had known only women for months. I wanted to cry, I wanted to bawl and weep. I just held him, let him hold me.

Until Steve said, "Come on, Dad. I can't hold this forever."

Molly got me out of there fast. I don't know how I would have gotten home on my own.

I had a message from Steve on the machine. "The doctor thought everything looked okay, but we won't know until we get the tests back. We'll call you then. In the meantime, have the decency to leave her alone."

After my mother was released from the hospital, Steve called me again, this time to lay down the new family guidelines. I was not welcome at family gatherings. I was not to inquire about my mother's health. Someone would notify me if there were any other emergencies, but I was to stay away. He told me I was no longer part of the family.

"Does Mom know you're doing this?" I asked. "Does Dad?"

"Just leave it alone, Molly. Mom's sick because of you, isn't that enough?"

Frankly, I wasn't totally convinced the cancer wasn't my fault, that one tiny dot of ice had not broken off and, instead of melting, solidified in her breast.

Molly saved my life then. I dragged myself to whatever job I had, whether recording or performing. My playing was listless and careless. I would come home and Molly would have some treat for me — either a meal she had cooked (and this was a sign of love, for she is not handy in the kitchen) or a little gift, a book, a tape. She gave me massages — and these truly relaxed me, for I knew that they, unlike those Jonathan had offered, would not be followed by coaxing and cajoling for something I didn't want.

I was only too happy to give myself to Molly then. Have not stopped being willing, but in those days sex for me was an affirmation, a reminder of who I was. When I caught myself obsessing about my family I rooted into Molly, into the life we were building. Our bed became a ship navigating waters frigid with icebergs. I didn't think about Baby then. Never stopped wanting one, but I had all I could handle in dealing with the loss of my family.

Cleaning was the best tonic for me. Our apartment gleamed during those days of battle. Once when Molly came home from her studio she found me on my hands and knees, naked, scrubbing the bathtub.

I looked up at her. "I was going to shower, but thought I'd do this first." Molly didn't care about explanations. She knelt beside me and started to kiss my neck. "I'm all sweaty," I protested. She tongued around my ear. "Moll, I've got Comet on my hands." She reached over and ran water in the tub, reached from behind me and put my hands under it. Her shirt felt soft against my back. "Your sleeves are getting wet." I pushed them up her arm. She moved her hands back to my body, played with my nipples as she kissed my back. Slowly, maddeningly slowly. I turned, hands dripping, and fumbled with the zipper of her pants while she moved her hands between my legs. "Help me," I said. But she was busy. I persisted. My wet fingers had soaked her shirt, made the cotton around the buttons thick and unmanageable. "Shit. I can't get this." Molly stilled my hand, pulled me down on top of her. Not at all slow then.

Her hands everywhere on me.

My mother's lump, though small, had been malignant, and she had to undergo chemotherapy. My father kept me posted. He started calling from work, once a month or so. He didn't talk about my mother except to fill me in on her recovery. He never mentioned Molly, or my being gay. I can't remember what he did talk about.

After almost a year he got my mother to come on the line. "Your father brought home a Mozart symphony. He says you played on it."

"First violin," I said.

"Good for you. Here's your father."

Except for a total absence of inflection and enthusiasm, and the fact that I hadn't heard my mother's voice in so long, this could have been a routine call.

We started talking more regularly after that. Our conversations were awkward and uneven. Sometimes she was almost civil, though not warm. Other times she would call me unnatural, selfish. The tone could turn at any moment; I had to be vigilant.

I kept my first forays to my parents' house brief. I'd arrive after dinner — they always ate at 6:30 — so I'd get there in time for coffee and to give my mother an excuse to fuss in the kitchen with the dishes while I sat with my father.

One night my father, in the middle of a card trick, whispered to me, "If anybody gives you any trouble, tell them to go to hell." He had yet to mention my being gay, had made no reference to Molly. But that night as I kissed him goodbye he told me to say hello to my friend for him.

My whole family didn't come back to me for two years, more because of what I didn't do than what I did. All I could do, with Molly's help, was wait them out. I continued to tell them I loved them, wanted to be with them, and would do so only if they were nice to me. Once my mother started yelling or making critical remarks I would leave. I had to leave for my own interests as well, since I wanted to stay and convince her, to make her see. I would no longer argue or defend or try to explain my life to anyone.

When I look back now I see that the fight about the Limoges on the night I came out to my mother offered a clue to the displaced arguments we would later have. After I started going back my mother fought with me about my career — how I was wasting my talent playing on pop recording sessions, how I mishandled the money I earned from those sessions, how I dressed, how I failed to take proper care of my car. Long after she accepted Molly into the family, included us in events and invitations, started giving Molly birthday and Christmas presents, talked to her on the phone, let her play with the grandchildren, she still never quite let me off the hook for being a lesbian.

Even now any stressful situation — her regular mammograms, my father's back surgery, their move to Oregon — can prompt carping phone calls. I remain her most convenient whipping girl.

My mother still loves me, but nothing I have

done since that day I came out to her has melted that tiny chunk of blue ice around her heart. I still wear sweaters when I go to see her, pack enough clothing to dress in layers. I wouldn't tell her about Baby because I refused to be pregnant under that chill. Just as she removed part of herself from me when I came out to her, so have I learned to keep a part of myself from her. When we go to see them I bring just the part of me that belongs to them. The rest of my life I leave at home.

It's fitting that Molly's family moved to Miami, with its almost tropical weather. I've never felt anything but warmth from them. They accepted me right away, welcomed me into the family. Ruth sends me cards on my birthday.

I still have a hard time being around Molly's family because they're so easy, were so easy, compared to my family. I'm still a little jealous of the Rubins' immediate acceptance of Molly, of how they press us eagerly about Baby.

I'm lying to all of them. To Molly's family because we haven't told them what a failure my trying to get pregnant has been, to my family because they don't know about my obsession these past three years.

To Molly also, because I will raise a child with or without her.

# *Molly*

When Molly walked into the living room at
six-thirty in the morning on her second day in
Miami, Ben was standing by the window in his
beach robe. His hair was wet.

"Morning, Dad. You already go for a swim?" This
was his vacation pattern, always a swim before
breakfast, when everyone else was still asleep. "Do
you want coffee?"

"If you're making some."

Molly measured water into the carafe. A few
minutes later she poured a mug for each of them.
"Don't rush him," Alix had advised the night before.
"See if he brings it up. If he doesn't, take your
time," she'd said. Ben picked up the sports section.
Molly didn't want to lose him there. "Have you
taken your walk yet?"

"No. Want to join me?"

As if she hadn't set her alarm for exactly that. "Sure."

They sat on the balcony letting their coffees cool. Ben's silence made Molly uncomfortable, so she rushed to fill it with words, a habit left over from years before when she'd felt compelled to remind her distracted parent that hey, not everyone had died. "Had we already planted the peach trees last time you were out?"

Ben couldn't remember.

"We had lots of fruit last year, but the birds got most of it."

Molly didn't know how to jump from peaches to what she really wanted to discuss, which was Ben's move. Alix had coached her the night before, but it was as if Ben's reticence was contagious. Soon Jerome would be out with them, and there would go her chance to talk to her father, to find out whatever possessed him to make this decision. Unaccustomed to personal discussions with him, Molly had never been able to come up with graceful transitions. She'd always just jump right in. *Hi, what's for dinner, I'm a lesbian. Great tie, Dad, how was your day, I'm moving to Los Angeles.*

She didn't know how to talk to her father about anything — his move or the baby or the mess with Alix. She could jumble it all together — *Don't move, I might need to come back to New York.* Put it into the form of a little joke, something to break the ice.

Before she could get anything out Jerome burst into the room singing "You Make Me Feel So

Young." He acted out the words like a nightclub singer, pointing at Ben and at Molly.

Ben put down his coffee and raised his hands to his lips to accompany Jerome on the second verse.

Molly sat back and smiled at her uncle.

They postponed exercise in favor of breakfast. Matzoth brei, Jerome's specialty.

"Is Alix up? She won't want to miss this," Jerome said, igniting the burner under a frying pan. "The key is to let it soak for a long time. I got up early to do that."

"Any of that lox left from yesterday?" Ben rummaged through the refrigerator.

"That was two days ago."

"It was? What was yesterday?"

"Corned beef and pastrami."

"That was yesterday? When did I get here?"

"Today's Friday. You got here Tuesday."

"The crab place?"

"Right. We finished the lox two days ago."

"Whenever, it was good."

"Sure it's good. Better than the deli on First Avenue. Who needs New York." Jerome slid a pat of butter into the frying pan. It sizzled. "You won't regret this move, Ben."

"Ruth claims it's harder to get around," Molly said.

"That's because she wasn't used to driving. Your father drives in New York. At least here he won't have to fight off car thieves," Jerome said.

Molly looked at Ben. "Dad?"

Ben sipped his coffee. "It was nothing."

Jerome poured the egg and matzoth mixture into the pan. "He had just parked at the hospital and gone into the lobby when he remembered he'd left something in the car. Two minutes he was gone. Right, Ben, two minutes?"

"Jerome —"

"So he goes back to the car and some punk's trying to get in the driver's door. Your father shouted at him and he left."

Molly turned to Ben. "You didn't tell me any of this."

"There's more," said Jerome. "He makes his rounds, goes back to his car, and the same punk's there — *inside* this time — and he's got the dash taken apart." Jerome shook the pan. "Your father went in one door and the guy slipped out the other."

"I almost had him, too," Ben said, closing his fingers around an imaginary neck.

"Are you nuts?" Molly asked.

"Your father chased him down the block."

Molly couldn't believe what she was hearing. "What would you have done if you'd caught him?"

"Given him what for," Ben said firmly.

"Right, Dad. Provided he didn't shoot you first." Molly shook her head. "Can't you just take cabs like everyone else?"

"Well, he won't have those problems down here," Jerome said.

"What problems?" Alix walked in, raised her eyebrows at Molly to ask how it went.

Molly just rolled her eyes, pulled out a chair for Alix.

"No problems," Ben said. "Let's eat."

As soon as Jerome sat down the phone rang. He

brought a portable phone to the table. "Ruth, we're just having breakfast. I made matzoth brei." He swung the mouthpiece away from his face and snuck a bite of food before informing Molly and Alix, "They want to know if you want to go with them this afternoon. They're doing a show." Receiver back down to speak. "Sure, they want to. No, Ben and I are playing tennis. Okay. I'll tell them." He rang off and laid the phone on the table. "They'll pick you up at three."

After a few minutes Ben turned to Molly, clearing his throat. "Do you have to get home right away?"

"Why?"

"Just wondering. I thought maybe you could come back with me, help start to clean out the apartment."

*No* was on its way past Molly's lips when Alix kicked her under the table.

"You could take anything you like," Ben offered. "I won't need much down here."

"What about all the rest?"

"Probably sell it. What do I need it for?"

Molly wasn't sure about needing it, but she did want it around, or to know that it was somewhere, preferably tucked in the same corner of the same shelf on the same bookcase it had sat on since she was in grade school. She turned to Alix, hoping for an out.

"I think it's a great idea," Alix said.

Molly's turn to deliver an under-the-table knock. Alix grinned at her.

"Good," Ben said. "I'll take care of the tickets today, see if I can get you on my flight."

131

Ben insisted on doing the dishes. Molly retreated with Alix to their bedroom. They each fluffed a pillow before pulling up her side of the sheets.

"I just don't know if it's the best thing for him to be doing."

"You want him to stay and work himself to death?"

"His work keeps him vital."

"You think his sisters aren't vital, or Jerome? Your father'll get into something here, if he ever comes off the tennis court."

"It's easy for you to joke about it. And what about my going to New York to pack up the place?"

"You don't think you should?"

"What about work?"

"Call your clients and tell them what's going on. You'll only be gone a few extra days."

Molly flopped onto the bed.

"What's your problem?" Alix asked. "You think if you don't go he won't move?"

"Maybe," Molly said.

"Can't you tell how happy he is here? It's good for him to be with his family. He's got his sisters and his brother —"

"Won't that be thrilling," Molly snapped.

"Grow up, Moll. Nothing stays the same."

Molly pulled Alix down next to her, put an arm around her. "We stay the same. We'll always stay the same."

"The last three years haven't changed us?"

"Nothing we can't fix now that we're getting back to normal." She nuzzled Alix's neck.

Alix pulled away, shifting to face her. "Meaning?"

"You know, once we get this stuff about Baby behind us."

Alix covered her face with both hands, bowed her head. When she looked up, her eyes were sad. "You haven't understood a thing about this 'stuff about Baby,' have you?"

"You always say that." She'd somehow wandered into a cloud, a heavy dream where someone was mad at her and she couldn't figure out why, but the anger wouldn't go away and the dream went on, never letting her off the hook. "I do understand. But now you're just upset because this last time didn't work. This is our chance to go on. We can have our life back."

"What did I just say about change? Molly, I love you, I love us, but this goes beyond us. I want a baby."

"What if you can't have one? You just tried everything under the sun —"

"I haven't tried adoption."

The cloud enveloped Molly. She couldn't wake herself up.

Alix said, "I'm going to call Carla when I get back."

"You can't. We never agreed —"

"At one point we agreed about having a baby. At least I thought we did. This is simply another way to do it."

"But —"

"What?"

"What if I say no?"

Alix appeared next to Molly on the cloud for one second, took a look around, looked into Molly's eyes in the cloud. "I'll do it with or without you, Molly."

Molly reached for her. "You're just upset because the last insemination didn't work."

Alix backed up a step. "I'm past upset, Molly. I'm going on. You can either catch up or stay behind."

No reeling her back this time.


The Girls picked Molly and Alix up at three sharp in a spiffy Dodge van. Ruth separated Pearl and Zelda whenever possible, so she drove with Pearl up front, and Molly wedged between Alix and Zelda in the back. Despite their physical proximity, Alix put as much distance between them as possible in the small space. She emitted a thin layer of frost.

Up front, Pearl and Ruth bubbled excitedly. Ruth's son David and his family and Pearl's son Les had arrived that morning, and both women were filled with news and updates. Francine, Pearl's daughter, would be landing any minute, and she'd brought her daughter and her granddaughter.

"So we'll be four generations at the party," Pearl beamed.

Ruth was frantic because she was making dinner for David and his family. "His grandchildren are the cutest, but they're such picky eaters, just like David used to be. I still have to buy something for dessert. I usually make something, but with everything that's been going on —"

Zelda interrupted. "If you knew they were coming, why did you schedule this performance?" She was in a black mood because of course her son Sam wouldn't show up.

"I told you. I didn't schedule it."

"So why are we here?" Zelda asked.

"The home got something mixed up and when they called to confirm I didn't have the heart to turn them down. Maybe it's better, everyone can unpack and settle in before tonight. The kids can go for a swim." She ventured a hurried glance away from the road, back at Molly. "Wait till you see the boys, Molly. You won't recognize them."

Molly had no doubt about that. She hadn't seen most of her first cousins in years, and had never even met many of their children.

"Thank God for freezers and microwaves," Ruth said. "I made brisket last week so all I have to do tonight is fix a vegetable. And get a dessert." Ruth kept up a nonstop chatter, talking about David and the kids, pointing out sights to Molly and Alix.

"I wish you had your violin, Alix, you could sit in with us," Pearl said.

"I'm happy to be in the audience for a change." Alix smiled, the first smile Molly had seen from her since that morning. The first time she'd seen her, really. If they'd had a chance to be in separate rooms, Alix took it. She talked to everyone but Molly. Except right before they went downstairs to meet the aunts, Alix had made it clear that she was staying in Miami for Ben, for his party. Fine, Molly had said. Fine, Alix had said. But it wasn't fine at all.

The home where the Girls were to perform was on Ocean Drive in an area called South Beach, a section that reminded Molly of California's Venice —

a funky-arty neighborhood undergoing major renovation. Across from a wide strip of public beach stood block after block of Art Deco buildings, many of them hotels that had been renovated. These sparkled trimly — all clean lines and glass block and fresh paint.

The home was neither Deco nor renovated. Seated outside on folding chairs, its residents, in their sandals and socks and windbreakers and little floppy hats, looked like caricatures of retired Miami seniors. The women wore brightly colored prints, the men mixed plaids and checks.

Zelda went inside to find the events coordinator while Molly and Alix helped Ruth and Pearl unload equipment — mike stands, keyboard, amplifier and speakers.

"This is quite a professional operation," Alix said as she secured a bungy cord around a speaker balanced on a collapsible luggage cart.

Zelda came out of the building with Sheila, a down-to-earth woman in her thirties, who led them through the lobby to an enclosed patio where rows of chairs were set up facing an empty space. A few people were already seated, and some watched from wheelchairs backed against the wall.

"I hope that's enough room for you," Sheila said. "I think this is how we did it last time."

"This is fine, darling," said Pearl.

Since Alix wasn't talking to her, Molly offered to help set up, but Ruth said they could manage, so Molly took a seat between Alix and a very thin woman in a wheelchair.

The enclosed patio gave the impression of being in a greenhouse, though one in which the few sad plants distributed around the area did not flourish. Everything looked a little battered, a little wilted from the heat and humidity.

The Girls were surprisingly efficient, considering how closely Zelda and Pearl had to work. Zelda and Ruth uncoiled wires and hooked everything up as Pearl warmed up the crowd.

She told them it was one of her baby brothers' birthdays. "We've only got two now, you know, our oldest, Saul, died years ago. And we lost our sister Rita this past year. Ben's here from New York and this is his daughter, our favorite niece — stand up, Molly — isn't she beautiful, all the way from California. And Alix, our other niece."

A smattering of applause greeted Molly and Alix's reluctant waves, and a thin palsied hand patted Molly's thigh.

After a sound check the Girls took their places, Pearl at the keyboard, Zelda and Ruth on her left and right. Without introduction Ruth set the beat and they launched with great gusto into "Begin the Beguine."

Molly had seen enough pictures the night before to be able to envision them all as they had been — Pearl the beauty, Ruth and Zelda plainer yet still strong and good-looking. She imagined them around the piano in their living room in the house in Brooklyn, the whole family then, with Rita and Saul and Ben and Jerome. Probably a few boyfriends, too, though with a family that large who needed anyone else for a party or a good time. They'd been singing for years, as kids, girls, young women, wives. This must have been the most natural thing in the world for them. Children and grandchildren, all the generations forgotten. Now they were The Girls again — forever young.

Ruth didn't start her patter until after the third song. She introduced her sisters and herself, then said, "It's a pleasure to be here. How's everyone doing today? Fine?" Lots of nods and some discussion from the audience. "It looked like you were just finishing your lunch when we got here." More nods from the crowd. "How was it? Good?"

"Okay," said one resident, a dapper chap in silk robe and leather slippers. "Baked chicken. Stewed prunes for dessert."

Which was all the prompting Pearl needed to launch into her *flomen* story, just as she'd told it the night before, which brought the same complaints from Zelda about the A&P. They were off and running. Ruth hit a button on her keyboard, a bouncy Latin beat kicked in, and she was into "Blame It On the Bossa Nova." In the best tradition of the show must go on, Pearl and Zelda stopped squabbling and joined in.

Molly was used to sitting through performances. She'd been to enough of Alix's over the years. Fiercely proud of Alix's talent, she had always found it an incredible turn-on to watch her perform. Once, driving home after a concert, she had detoured to the top of Mulholland Drive.

"What are you doing?" Alix had asked.

"I can't wait any longer," Molly said, yanking the emergency break and pulling Alix to her. The San Fernando Valley sparkled beneath them, but they were oblivious, and soon their windows were just as fogged as those of the other cars parked nearby.

Those days were gone, Molly thought, sitting in

that enclosed patio watching her aunts perform. Alix, as far from her as possible, might as well have stayed home for all the connection they had. Passion was a thing of the past, and not just sexual passion. Even Alix's music had become just work to her now, passion reserved for one thing only.

Molly was actually relieved that the day of the party had finally arrived. Alix wouldn't talk to her unless they were with other people.

"Come on, honey," Molly would plead when they had a minute to themselves. "Let's work this out."

"Do you want to raise a child?"

"Alix . . ."

"If the answer's yes, we have lots to talk about. If not, there's nothing to discuss."

When Molly remembered Alix's mention of calling Carla about adoption, she said, "Promise you won't call her till I get back."

"Why?"

"So you and I can discuss it first."

"What is there to discuss?"

"Just wait till I get back from New York."

"Molly, what's the difference? You think you can talk me out of this?"

"Just promise."

"I don't see the point."

"It's only a few days. What's a few days after all this time?"

Only after much discussion and pleading did Molly get Alix to agree not to call Carla. Stopgap only, not a solution, but she'd bought herself some time. Some very expensive time. As much as she didn't want to go to New York the next day, she knew she couldn't take much more of Alix the Ice Queen.

The festivities were going to be in the common room of Zelda's building, so no one's apartment needed cleaning. The caterers were taking care of the food. There would be none of Pearl's famous chopped liver or Zelda's herring so Molly was not needed for frantic last-minute runs to the supermarket. She had nothing to do.

She had planned for free time, imagining a long stroll on the beach with Alix, a few lazy hours on the sand, a nap in the afternoon, a little romance. Instead, Molly longed for errands to keep her busy, for myriad little details to dislodge the two huge blocks in her head: the loss of New York and, if she didn't shape up and go along with what had been their dream of starting a family, the possible loss of Alix.

In the car after their show Ruth had said, "With all the excitement of the birthday and your father's move, we haven't even talked about your baby."

"There's no baby yet, Aunt Ruth."

"Just wait," Pearl had said. "It'll seem like there never was a time without one."

Molly had always imagined, when she could jump that far ahead, bringing the baby to New York, introducing her to the doormen, to Patsy and Caroline, her father's receptionist and nurse. She had envisioned Baby crawling on the living room rug — the old cool dark Persian that had been her grandfather's — while she or Alix snatched ashtrays and vases out of the way of Baby's little round arms. In New York, Baby would either sleep with them in Molly's old room or, when older, in Michael's room. Baby would have a set of toys at the apartment, left there between visits. As Baby grew Molly would pull out old games — Chinese checkers, Chutes and Ladders, Monopoly — and books. Molly would read to Baby about horses and koala bears.

She couldn't put her finger on when the change had started, the progression from dream to excitement to fear and this final dread that kept her from saying yes to Alix.

Alix was down by the pool. Molly wandered into their bedroom, picked up Alix's atomizer and spritzed a jet of perfume into the air. She walked into the fine mist, an invisible cloud of Alix. If she closed her eyes she could pretend for one instant that Alix, the one she wanted, was next to her.


Ben insisted on driving to the party: "I've got to start learning my way around town." Jerome navigated. Molly sat as far into her back corner as possible in a vain effort to ignore Alix's presence on the seat next to her.

The streets weren't too crowded, which Molly deemed a good thing, since Ben was wandering in his lane.

"Dad, move over a little."

"I'm right in my lane."

"No, you're not."

141

"You sound just like Jerome. The dividers line up with the middle of the hood." A blue van whizzed by them, a sharp blast from its horn trailing behind. "What's he complaining about?"

"Dad, I could have peeled the decal off his rear bumper. Move a little to the left."

Molly used to feel so safe when her father drove. He'd gotten them through everything — blizzards, torrential rains, hailstorms, fog. Growing up, she believed he had a different view of the road because even when she couldn't see through the weather Ben kept the car moving forward — how could he do that, she reasoned, unless his position in the driver's seat afforded him a vision she didn't have.

She'd outgrown that perception but not some general sense of her father's omnipotence. Any lapse in that strength shocked her. She was still unused to seeing him as less than perfect, certainly to seeing him as a seventy-five-year-old. Her friends talked about their parents differently than Molly did, using their age — "Father's seventy-six," or "Mother's seventy-four" — as an excuse for their concern. As if that made them old. Though some of the people at the home the Girls sang at must have been Ben's age, Molly couldn't judge aging. When she told people how old Ben was, that he still worked full time, they were amazed. And she felt that same amazement — he was invincible. He'd proven that years ago, before she had moved to L.A.

That had been another birthday, his sixtieth. Molly and her lover at the time had celebrated with him at La Caravelle, an elegant French restaurant.

The phone had rung early the next morning.

Molly groped for the receiver, fumbled it to her ear without lifting her head from the pillow.

"Did I wake you?"

Her father's voice sounded as groggy as Molly felt. They'd finished a bottle of champagne at dinner. Molly looked toward the windows. It was still dark outside.

Next to her, Paula mumbled incoherently, shifted, still asleep. "What time is it?"

"Six-thirty."

"What's going on, Dad?"

"I'm going to the hospital."

*He's a doctor, he always goes to the hospital. Why is he telling me this at six-thirty in the morning?* She couldn't throw off the sleep settling around her.

"The ambulance will be here soon."

Molly bolted up, wide awake. "What's wrong? Who's going with you?"

"You are."

She arrived just as the paramedics were wheeling Ben out of his building. They had placed an oxygen mask over his face.

"What is it?" Molly was frantic, panicked.

"Seems like he's had a heart attack, miss." They lifted Ben into the ambulance. Molly climbed in next to him. She clung to his steel gurney as the ambulance careened up First Avenue.

Ben lifted the mask and murmured, "Here, give this to them." He waved some folded bills toward the paramedic in the front seat.

"No, Doc, keep your money," the man said in a Brooklyn accent.

But Ben kept waving it around until Molly took

the bills and handed them to the man. "It's my birthday," Ben said.

"Happy birthday, Doc."

Molly didn't cry at the hospital. Not when they wheeled Ben into the CICU and slammed the door in her face when she tried to follow. Not when, four minutes later, someone opened the same door — she still stood there in disbelief — and thrust a plastic bag against her chest. In the bag were Ben's wallet, wedding ring (even though Claire had been dead five years), gold necklace (Claire probably turned over in her grave when he first put that on), his bills in the money clip, some loose change. They'd also given her his shoes.

Still Molly didn't cry. She did pace the hall, at the far end of which was a pay phone. She must have walked to it a million times. But she couldn't call anyone because then she would cry. Then it would be true that Ben was in there, maybe dying.

Molly stayed in that hall for two hours before she called, in order, her father's office, Jerome, and her girlfriend Paula.

A few tears threatened to sneak out then, but she kept them back, pausing long moments between sentences. Ben was okay. It wasn't a heart attack. It was pericarditis.

She spent the day in a fog. She didn't go home until late that afternoon. The first thing she did was shower. She turned the hot down too far by mistake. The cold water pounded her and she wanted to escape, jump out of the water, but really she wanted to jump out of the present and into that moment twelve hours earlier when she'd been blissfully asleep and oblivious. She readjusted the faucet, too much hot this time, and she sprang away from the scalding water that gave her the excuse for the tears that finally came, that doubled her over in the dry end of the stall, crying in the steam and the spray, sobbing for someone, though she knew that without Ben there would be no one.

Ben's cardiologist, Dr. Howitt, gave Molly a long involved explanation about pericarditis. "It's very manageable. Don't worry." She explained that pericarditis was an inflammation of the pericardium, the membrane surrounding the heart. "Its symptoms resemble those of a heart attack — chest pain that moves to the shoulder or neck, breathing difficulty, sweat, chills, and physical collapse — that's why the CICU team handled it so aggressively. But it wasn't a heart attack." Maybe it was caused by a virus, no one could be sure.

The medical explanations meant little to Molly. The doctors could tell her all they wanted to about this virus and that infection, about diet and exercise. Molly knew better. She'd watched Ben ever since Claire died. She'd been watching him long before that, had watched them both, since Michael. Trying to learn how they coped. And all she'd seen was Ben at work, Ben taking calls during dinner, going back to the hospital after dinner, stopping to make a house call on the way. Ben allowed no one into his life after Claire — not his brother, not the women he dated. So something like this, Molly thought, was inevitable. Fourteen years after Michael's death and five years after Claire's, Ben couldn't take it anymore. Dr. Howitt could call it what she would, but Molly knew it was Ben's heart breaking. She knew this deep in her own fragile heart.

Ben had frequent relapses for the next four or five years — especially around holidays. Dr. Howitt badgered him to slow down. He wasn't giving himself time to heal properly, she said, that's why it always came back.

Either Ben's heart had mended or scarred over, for eventually the bouts stopped. By then they had become routine, less scary. Ben could predict them, and he'd pack a bag and off he'd go to the hospital.

He refused to wear pajamas or hospital gowns — someone might think he was sick — and Molly would bring him chinos and polo shirts and clean socks from home. Friends and patients would bring him food, and not just the usual boxes of candy.

Once when Molly showed up Ben asked if she was hungry. "You've got your choice," he said. "Mrs. Spagnoli dropped off homemade lasagna, Mrs. Bergman chicken soup. We've got corned beef from the Carnegie Deli, bagels and lox from Zabar's. And there's fruit. And cookies."

"No ice cream?" she joked.

"There's Häagen-Daz in the freezer at the nurse's station."

The hospital stays became episodes of the stories she told about her father, part of the legend of invincibility she'd built for him. Everyone laughed at what a character Ben was.

He'd had no recurrence for almost ten years and the hospital stories seemed archaic, part of another era. Molly rarely told them anymore, but under no circumstances, if Ben's pericarditis was ever referred to, did she mention the terror of that ambulance ride, or the sharp fear and utter loneliness of her vigil in the corridor outside the CICU.

Besides, here he was, driving to his birthday party, seventy-five and healthy and about to make a major change in his life. Molly watched his hands on the wheel. Brown spots showed through the thick dark hair, nails still manicured and buffed. When had she last touched her father's hands? She didn't know. She imagined they would be amazingly pink-palmed as always — abd smooth and dry, but she couldn't know for sure.

They arrived a few minutes early, but already about thirty people had shown up. A sound system blared one of the many tapes Jerome had made for the evening, a mix of show tunes, big band, Frank Sinatra. The entrance was draped with streamers and a droopy Happy Birthday banner. Inside, helium balloons stroked the ceiling, drifted in the breeze from the open patio doors leading to the pool. The long strings from the balloons caressed the heads of the guests, grazed a cheek, a bald spot.

Jerome grabbed Alix and took her to inspect the sound system, to make sure his tapes were in order. Standing next to Ben, Molly acclimated herself to the scene. She didn't know half these people — some were friends of her aunts, some former patients of her father's who had already retired to Miami, some had made the trip especially for the occasion. She figured she was related to the other half, though. When her aunts had moved to Miami, the center had been pulled out of family event-planning, and get-togethers were rare. Molly wouldn't recognize most of her second cousins if she met them on the street. She'd heard through the aunts who had children, which grandchildren had children, but she didn't bother to remember the names. Now the room was crawling with adults and children and Molly didn't know which of them were related to her.

Someone snatched Ben from her, so she stood alone. But only for a moment. People she didn't know came up to her and told her, "Ben doesn't look a day over sixty." None of them could believe how well he looked, how healthy he was, that he still practiced full time. "And I bet he still makes house calls, right?" they'd say. Molly smiled at all of them.

Two little boys zoomed past her to chase balloons. Every time they snagged one they would run excitedly to Ruth, who would interrupt her conversation briefly to beam proudly at them. For a moment Molly thought they must be her cousin David's sons. Then with a shock she realized they were his grandchildren.

At last Molly spotted someone she recognized — David, Ruth's oldest son, a financial consultant. His wife, Myra, was a buyer for Bloomingdales. Consummate New Yorkers, they ate in restaurants where even with a reservation you waited an hour for your table. They knew where to shop, where to vacation, where to find the best fruits out of season.

David and Myra stood a few feet from Molly, making no attempt to hide their disinterest in what Les, Pearl's son, was saying to them.

Les had been a stockbroker until he had a nervous breakdown. He left his job, his seat on the stock exchange, his wife, his home in Scarsdale, and moved to Vermont to find himself. "He shouldn't have much trouble doing that," David had said, "Vermont's small." Les had been through lots of therapy, gotten in touch with his anger, tried to live a simpler life. He never wore suits anymore and owned several pair of Birkenstock sandals. There was a rumor in the family that he was dating a much younger woman.

They all stopped talking when Molly approached. "Hello, cousin," David said, opening his arms.

Molly hugged him, Myra, Les. "Hello, cousins."

"Where's Alix?" Myra asked.

Molly gestured vaguely. "Around somewhere," she said. The two little boys zoomed by. "Look, Grandma, balloons!"

Myra looked at Molly. "I hear soon you'll have one of your own."

Molly smiled as vaguely as she'd gestured. She turned to David. "Do you know which ones we're related to? Aside from those two, of course. It's easy to see the resemblance." Molly pointed to the balloon-chasers.

"Zach and Max. Quite a handful. It's much easier dealing with them as a grandfather."

"I can imagine," Molly said. "Where are . . ." She blanked at the names of his sons.

"Peter's around here somewhere," Myra said. "John couldn't get away — he's trying to make partner so all he does is work."

"How've you been, Les?" Molly asked.

"Okay," he answered. "I've been pretty involved in the men's movement."

David suggested that that must be great for attracting women. "These days they're all looking for sensitive men," he said. Les said that picking up women was not the point of the movement. David and Myra both stifled yawns.

Molly had always liked Les. He was the same age as Michael; David was five or six years older.

Les and Michael had been very close. After Michael died, Les had tried to keep in touch with her, writing to her sometimes from college, visiting when he came to New York. She rarely wrote back. Growing up, she had never talked to either Les or David at parties because the age difference seemed so vast. Now they were lumped together in the same generation. Both men (men? When had that happened to her cousins, these boys who had been like Michael, the same age, smooth-cheeked darlings, racing around family gatherings all disheveled and untucked like David's grandsons today?) had aged well in typical Rubin fashion. Les had dark wavy hair flecked with gray and a neatly trimmed beard and mustache. David's hair was thinning but an expensive cut made the most of what was left. And here he was, with sons and grandsons, the proud papa, successful businessman. And Les, a newly licensed therapist, living apart from his family, was beginning a second life. What would have become of Michael?

"Good, they've started serving," David said. "I'm starved."

Two long tables piled with catered food graced one corner. David, Myra and Les wandered over to join the line.

Molly looked around for Alix, spotted her with Pearl's daughter, Francine, who was the center of an admiring group of aunts and their friends. Francine held her granddaughter, a smiling, round, good-natured baby, daughter of her daughter Tracy. Tracy was in high school the last time Molly had seen her.

Molly didn't think of Francine as being old enough to be a grandmother. But then she did some figuring and realized Francine had to be over fifty.

Francine was just passing the baby to Alix, everyone cooing at the baby, Pearl smiling knowingly, reassuringly at Alix, as if to say, "You're next." Molly thought she could skip that group.

She looked around for her father. He was surrounded by his brother and sisters and a well-dressed woman who seemed to have eyes only for him. Or maybe for Jerome. She appeared quite friendly with both, listening intently when they spoke, laughing at their jokes. She showed her interest by placing a hand on Ben or Jerome's forearm to emphasize a point, or playfully swatting at that forearm, the gesture accompanied by a little giggle and a flirty, dismissive "Oh, you don't mean that."

Molly watched, fascinated, until Pearl swept her up and said, "I want you to meet someone." But instead of whisking her off in the opposite direction Pearl steered her straight to her father and this woman. "Lou, here she is." Under her breath to Molly: "She's wanted to meet you, too."

The woman extended her hand for a polite shake, but as soon as Pearl said, "This is Ben's daughter," the woman lunged forward and grabbed both Molly's hands in one of those pseudo-sincere gestures.

"So *good* to meet you, Molly," she said. Huge emphasis on the *good*. "I've heard so much about you from everyone."

Pearl beamed, saying to no one in particular, "I

knew you'd just love her. Molly, this is Mrs. Steinmetz, the best real estate agent in Miami Beach."

"Call me Louise, please," said Mrs. Steinmetz, still clutching Molly's hands. "I'm going to find your Dad a great place." She added conspiratorially, "And I'll make sure your room has a view of the ocean."

Zelda saved Molly from coming up with a reply by nudging her heartily in the ribs. "Look how cute!" She elbowed her again. "Poke Ruth, she's gotta see this." Molly looked where Zelda pointed.

Francine's group had grown, and Alix still stood in its center with the baby.

Zelda grabbed Molly's arm and dragged her through the circle. "Here we come. Francine, look who's here."

Big greetings from Francine, who relished another chance to show off her granddaughter. Molly enthused about the baby.

Francine said, "Here, hold her."

"Oh, I don't —"

"Yes, Molly, you're going to have to get used to this. She's already taken quite a shine to Alix," Ruth said, taking the baby from Alix and putting it in Molly's arms before she could protest.

The baby didn't seem too pleased and started squirming and crying at once. No one seemed at all concerned, certainly not Tracy, clear across the room at the buffet, obviously relieved to have all those relatives to spell her for an evening.

"Look how cute, Alix. Don't you wish you had a picture of that?" Ruth asked.

Alix didn't have to answer because Francine

dragged her and the others off to the buffet table, leaving Molly alone with the baby.

Molly looked down at this tearful bundle in her arms and tried not to seem afraid. She'd heard horses sensed a rider's fear — did babies have the same innate ESP? She was amazed at the baby's ability to change the impression of her weight, to become so difficult to hold. When people held babies they never let on what a challenge it was, or what the secret was, the special knack everyone else seemed to have for keeping it, if not quiet, at least still. Was she going to be stuck with this difficult bundle all night?

She needn't have worried. Before too long another admiring grandmother came along and expertly took the baby from her. Molly gratefully moved to the buffet, but an impression of that surprising weight lingered in her arms.

A kids' table had been set up at one end of the room. Molly realized with a shock that she didn't belong at it. Her generation were the parents now. She sat between Ben, the birthday boy, and Zelda. Pearl was on Ben's other side, next to Jerome. Ruth sat on Zelda's other side, Alix next to her.

Throughout the meal, no matter what the topic, Molly would be listening or speaking and suddenly a sharp elbow in her ribs, a harsh whisper — "Poke your father. Poke your father." David's grandsons playing with the balloons. Francine, Tracy and the baby posing for a photograph. Zelda kept so busy monitoring the activities in the room that Molly held her arm near her side in a vain effort to prevent bruises.

Midway through the meal David stood to make a toast to Ben. He had composed a witty family history, chronicling his grandparents' arrival in America, settling in Brooklyn, opening their first dress shop, the brownstone in East New York, the closeness of all the brothers and sisters even today.

Molly watched Alix as David spoke. She seemed to be paying attention. Hell, maybe she was, she seemed to be moved in all the right places — obviously Molly couldn't read her at this point. Normally they'd sit together at a family function, sit together and hold hands under the table, or above the table, refer to each other in conversation, second each other's thoughts and comments. Tonight they hadn't even made eye contact.

By the time David finished there wasn't a dry eye in the room. He raised his glass. "To family." Everyone echoed his words and drank.

Molly drank too, even though she didn't know anymore what family was. She didn't understand when Ruth clutched her to her breast, or when the others made such a fuss over her. Why did family think they were entitled to some piece of her simply because they were related? Each aunt claimed her traits as her own. "She got that from me," Pearl would say. "I was always artistic. I could spend hours in a museum." "You never —" "Zelda Traub, yes, I did."

Molly watched her cousins with their kids, grown and growing, and wondered about the sacrifices they'd made or were willing to make, experiences they'd had. Tried to imagine if she could do that.

This was part of growing up that she hadn't completed.

Maybe Alix was right. Maybe she'd never grown up.

Jerome cranked up the volume on the stereo and led Pearl onto the dance floor. Molly had heard so many times how Pearl wanted to be a dancer but Poppa wouldn't let her. She was graceful as ever at eighty-five. Ben and Ruth stepped out, and Zelda dragged Les with her.

Molly could hear Zelda over the music, "Poke Ruth! Poke Pearl!" She pointed to where David's grandsons were dancing in a corner, all jerky and bouncy. But no one paid attention for long because a Charleston played and the Rubins went wild, shaking and kicking. Molly had forgotten Les was such a good dancer. Everyone circled around, clapping and cheering them on. Even the kids were drawn to the circle.

David stood next to Molly. "How many octogenarians do you know who can moonwalk?" he asked, pointing to Pearl.

The aunts were truly amazing. A little hip-hop mixed in with the turkey trot or the black bottom, any step just as long as they were moving. Jerome strutted and kicked. Even Ben — he may not have been a talker but he sure could dance.

Molly remembered a period when her parents took lessons. A dark Latin American couple had come to the apartment to teach them the hot dances at the time — mambo, samba, merengue, rumba. Molly sometimes was allowed to stay up to watch. It was the kind of memory she wouldn't trust if she hadn't had evidence — the man scarred the dining room table with his lit cigarette while demonstrating a step. The black burn mark was still there.

David danced with Francine because Myra was dancing with Peter, her oldest son. Zelda had moved on to another guest.

Les approached Molly. "Come on, cousin."

"You're too good for me."

"Come on." Les held out his arms.

Molly looked around for Alix, thinking she'd offer her as substitute. Alix loved to dance, though they never went to the clubs anymore. Their dances were limited to brief spins around the living room or short swirls like the one that had ended in the dip in the kitchen.

A few months earlier, Molly had surprised Alix by suggesting they stop at the Palms before heading home after a play. They parked close by on Santa Monica Boulevard and walked hand-in-hand down the steps of the only permanent women's bar in West Hollywood.

They headed straight for the dance floor to catch the end of a slow song. When it ended, they stayed for the next number, a big dance hit. They separated for that one. Molly kept time in place, trying to remember how she used to dance. Alix got into the music right away. More women crowded the floor. Alix inched closer. Molly moved back. Alix shimmied still closer. Again Molly retreated.

Finally Alix held Molly, spoke loudly in her ear to be heard above the music. "Why do you keep backing off? I'm trying to be sexy here."

"Oh. I thought you needed more room."

Alix had laughed, grabbed her, and spun them around. "Moll, it's been way too long between dances."

Luckily the dance with Les was brief. The girls had been persuaded to do a few songs from their act. They opened with "Happy Birthday," followed by a special song Ruth had written for Ben to the tune of "It's Delovely." A tribute to Ben's life and medical career, the chorus was "He's de doctor." Next, a logical segue, "You're the Tops."

Ben stood uncomfortably alone while his sisters sang to him. About thirty seconds into the first song he took Molly's wrist and pulled her next to him. Molly looked at the faces around them, eager, smiling, wincing at a particularly bad pun. She was as uncomfortable as Ben inside that circle. She instinctively found Alix's face for support, but at that moment those features she knew better than her own held nothing for her. She focused on each sister, good-natured and earnest, beaming with unconditional love for their brother. She passed to the patients she recognized, ones who had become friends over the years, inviting Ben down for vacations, a week, a weekend, any time he could spare. She felt her father next to her, squirming under all the attention, but happy, finally. Peaceful, that's how he looked here. She took his hand. It was just as she'd remembered it, dry and smooth, the dark hair softer than it looked. She'd forgotten how warm it was.

And in that moment, just as her aunts were winding up their song, Molly knew that Ben had found his place. Alix had been right. Leaving New York and moving to Florida was absolutely right for him. No Michael, no Claire — where else would he go? Here he was surrounded by his brother and sisters, his new Miami friends. For the first time since Claire died Ben was doing something good for himself.

When everyone sang "Happy Birthday" Molly cried. She knew people would think she was touched by the occasion, and she was, but really she was crying for New York, and for herself. For just as Ben was settling into his place she was being yanked out of hers.

No one could persuade Ben to make a speech, though he did thank everyone for coming.

Jerome helped him out. "My big brother's always been shy." He recounted their adventure in the nightclub, so Ben had a chance to demonstrate his whistling prowess.

There was more dancing after that until the party wound down. But this did not mean a trickle of guests leaving for home. Everyone went at once. Suddenly the party was over. The brothers and sisters kissed one another goodnight, as if they were still part of the same family, not now heads of their own lines. Their children and grandchildren left for their hotels, and the brothers and sisters were together again — as it should be — Molly's presence the only evidence that life had ever been any different.

Back at Jerome's, Ben and Jerome rooted in the refrigerator as they rehashed the party.

"Molly, Alix, want anything?" Ben asked.

"No, thanks." She kissed her uncle goodnight, then her father. "Happy birthday, Pop." She hugged Ben. Then Alix hugged him too. "Happy Birthday, Ben."

He kissed them each and they marched off to their room.

"It's freezing in here," Molly said, unbuttoning her shirt. She slipped off the shirt, her bra, hurriedly yanked on a T-shirt. She folded her pants over a chair, peed, brushed her teeth. She and Alix had lived together long enough that their rhythms fit. Alix used the bathroom while Molly undressed, undressed while Molly was in the bathroom. They usually made it to bed at the same time. "Aren't you cold?" Molly asked as she climbed into bed next to Alix.

"No." Alix turned off the lamp beside the bed.

"I thought it was a pretty good party," Molly said. "I think I'm going to be bruised tomorrow. Did Zelda jab you? Turn on the light, I want to see if I'm black and blue."

The room popped back from the dark. Alix didn't turn toward Molly.

Molly checked her side. "Nothing yet." In the dark again. "I'm stuffed. Can you imagine if my aunts had cooked? 'Try this, I made it. Don't try that, Pearl made it.' The pressure would have been unbearable."

"Look," said Alix, a cold voice in the dark. "If you want to have this ridiculous conversation I will. We can pretend nothing's wrong, we can pretend we still want the same things. Would you like that? I tried as long as I could. I gave you the benefit of the doubt. But let's not play games, okay?"

"Don't you think we should talk about this?"

"We're past words now. Let's just go to sleep."

A thousand unspoken protests later Molly knew Alix was awake, even though neither of them had moved. Molly wished she could retreat into sleep, wished she could hear the ocean. She pictured it, this silent repetition of blue turning to white, swell to wave to spume, tumbling onto the beach, raking back, endlessly repeating its silent drumming. Facts of her life were thrown up on the sand, displayed, then erased by the tide, so that with each step she was forced to examine her options over and over. The waves posed one problem, cleared it, revealed another. Baby, no baby. The possibility of losing Alix, and losing New York. It didn't matter — the waves erased each one, leaving her a blank slate impossible to inscribe with any degree of certainty.

Molly opened her eyes, unaware of having slept, ignorant for one moment of the cause of the heaviness in her limbs. Then she heard Alix step out of the bathroom and she remembered everything. She sat up, reached for her watch. Alix, naked except for a towel around her wet hair, efficiently stuffed socks around the edge of the clothes she'd already packed.

"What are you doing?"

Alix didn't answer, just looked at her for a second before turning back to her bag.

"Your plane doesn't leave until noon. It's only six-thirty."

"I'm going to wait at the airport."

"But we're going to drive you."

"I'll call a cab." Alix yanked the suitcase off the dresser and set it by the door.

The incongruity of Alix's naked body and the suitcase made Molly want to smile, to make a joke, but she knew better. Once Alix got an idea into her head — talk about stubborn.

"You're going to spend the whole morning at the airport?"

Alix stepped into the bathroom, unwrapping the towel from her head. Molly watched her reflected in the mirror as she shook out her hair, then combed it. "I'll leave you the toilet kit," Alix said into the mirror. She plugged in the dryer. Her light brown hair looked darker when wet, and the effect of that, plus seeing her mirror image — brush in the wrong hand, ring on the wrong hand — made Alix look like someone else, a stranger masquerading as Alix.

Molly said, "I wish you'd stay," but the whine of the dryer drowned out her words. Just as well, what would a few more hours together do? Prolong the discomfort. Cause another fight, or let the one that had been bubbling since their arrival finally come to a boil.

Molly got out of bed to pee and wash her face and hands, navigating around Alix in the tiny space. She slipped into sweatpants and a T-shirt before flopping back onto the bed. They weren't home, she couldn't sulk in another room, hide outside, walk the dog. She had to watch every familiar step — Alix drying her hair, putting on face cream, body lotion — all her actions brisk and capable. Underwear, loose white cotton shirt, tan slacks, socks and shoes.

Molly imagined grabbing Alix, hauling her down on the bed, straddling her to make her stay, to force her to listen. *I went along with you, now you go along with me. Give us a chance.*

When Alix was dressed she slung her backpack over one shoulder, hefted her suitcase. "See you in four days."

Molly stood between her and the door. She looked into Alix's blue, blue eyes that were open to her still, but for how much longer? She reached for Alix's hand. All motion hers, all energy, it took all her own effort to bring the hand to her lips. Alix wouldn't give her an inch.

Molly gave it one more try. "Don't leave like this." This time she meant it. Alix's eyes filled with tears. Molly kissed Alix's palm, bowed her head into the gesture.

"Say it, Molly. 'I want a baby.' "

"Come on, Alix . . ."

"That's all I need to hear."

"Alix, there's New York and my father's move. Can't we do this when I get back?"

"What's there to do? I'm just asking you to say something, here and now. You don't have to do anything."

"This is very stressful for me."

Alix had been holding her suitcase the whole time. Her backpack had slid down her arm, she'd caught it and it hung from her other hand, hindering her movement when she reached for the doorknob. "Could you open that for me, please."

"Alix . . ."

"Never mind, I'll get it." She hefted her backpack up her arm and reached for the knob. Molly clasped her hand over Alix's, ready to do anything to make her stay, because if she walked out now, like this,

Molly didn't know if she could get her back. "Alix —" The silence more demanding than words. "What if it's just not what I want?"

Hand gone, Alix gone, bags gone. Only perfume remained, sharp on Molly's tongue, in her nostrils. And emptiness bigger than any room could ever measure.

Molly fled to the beach — down in the same elevator Alix must have taken, because here too Alix's perfume lingered. Molly kept pounding the button to make the car go faster, to bang Alix's last words out of her head. "Three years, Molly, three years and you couldn't tell me the truth?"

Molly's hair frizzed in the humid air. It felt like someone else's hair, like a hat. But then everything seemed a little tricky, a little off. Still, anything was better than staying in the empty room after Alix left. Anything would have been preferable to her leaving.

She wanted a windswept beach, cliffs, fog. A Northern California or Oregon beach, desolate and rugged. Here, the air was a pleasant temperature though the humidity made it thick. The surf was gentle, more pacific than the Pacific, and a clean sweet blue. The receding tide left a treasure for beachcombers, and the waves washing over the wide band of shells made them tinkle like coins. Molly stooped and gathered some. Several were delicately lined, reminiscent of blue veins under china skin. Others displayed intricate filigree, lacy webbing. She liked the sharp crunch of them underfoot. She plucked a miniature conch from the water. If she held it up to her ear, would it reveal tiny secrets to her? Just one or two small answers?

Out of habit she'd collected several to bring to Alix. Useless now. She tossed them all back, the conch as well as a delicately patterned herringbone and three vivid yellow shells the size of a baby's fingernail.

She heard music as she came down the corridor. Artie Shaw and his orchestra playing "Things Are Looking Up." Ben must have plugged in the boom box she gave him and cranked up the volume all the way. She walked in to find him and Jerome, in sweats and T-shirts, playing with Ben's presents. Ben had already donned an assortment of his gifts: a white tennis hat like the one Jerome had worn to the airport, a yellow *Father Knows Best* cardigan — very out of character for Ben, who only wore pullovers — a paisley tie draped around his neck. Tags hung off his sleeve and over his left ear.

"Morning, Moll," Jerome called, a little breathless from dancing around the living room.

Ben read a card from Ruth, then tore into her package. "I know what this is," he said as he pulled a perpetual-motion sculpture out of the box. He had a fascination for these wire formations that sat like seesaws on a fulcrum. The slightest nudge set them moving, they'd roll and pitch side to side indefinitely. His sisters always gave him one or two, whatever the occasion. Ben had dozens of them in his office. Sometimes Molly would get them all going at once, a glinting distracting backdrop against which Ben sat motionless.

"Alix still asleep?" Ben asked.

"She left." Molly tried to sound as casual as possible.

"Is everything all right?"

"Fine," Molly lied. "She checked her machine last night and had a call for a double session with a solo or something so she changed her flight. She said to say goodbye."

Neither her father nor her uncle questioned the story. If Molly pretended, she might even believe it herself.

"You know, Ben," said Jerome, "you shouldn't even bother taking this stuff back to New York. You'd just have to pack it twice."

"It wouldn't be in your way here?"

"Not at all. I might even wear that sweater."

Ben continued to open presents. More ties, another tennis sweater, knickknacks and kitchen gadgets. For years he had talked about taking up cooking. He subscribed to at least three food magazines, had all the *Time/Life* cookbooks. Still, he never got further than his one specialty, scrambled eggs on Saturday or Sunday mornings.

"Remember this, Ben?" Jerome stood bouncing in time to the beat of the next tune, Artie Shaw's clarinet blowing cool and swingy. " 'Bedford Drive.' Come on." Jerome grabbed Molly and led her around the room, but he got too fancy for her and picked Ben up on his next pass by the couch. The two brothers danced together. "See, Moll, watch," Jerome said as he and Ben effortlessly spun and turned in the paper-strewn living room.

"Just like Fred and Ginger," Molly said.

"Ready for your turn?"

"Think I'll just shower."

Even behind the closed door of her room Molly could hear the music, something snaky now. And like a snake slithering its way up a tree, Alix's perfume wrapped itself around Molly. She stepped into the shower and scrubbed her skin raw in a futile attempt to erase the scent. It was as strong as memory.

Three hours later she was dragging behind Ben and Jerome down the corridor of yet another high-rise on Collins Avenue. Another hallway with mirrors and patterned wallpaper and decor so unlike Molly's taste that she couldn't quite focus on any of it. There was no place for her eye to settle between the gilt and the plush and the lucite and the mirrors. She could no longer distinguish the first place from the fourth. Which one had the ocean views? Which the tiny closets? This was the fifth or sixth unit Mrs. Steinmetz — "Call me Louise" — had shown them.

Molly was pretty sick of it by now. Sick of the similar apartments, sick of tropical Miami, sick of her father and Jerome flirting with Mrs. Steinmetz.

At least it was cool inside. The morning's mild humidity had blossomed into a thick weight. Molly spent the hunt in a constant sticky state, her shirt clinging to her back. She resented Mrs. Steinmetz for staying so cool-looking, for keeping her gait so bouncy.

Mrs. Steinmetz jangled her set of keys as she walked briskly down another corridor redolent of brisket and chicken soup, the heavy air of the holidays. Parked outside one door was a neon-pink tricycle, surely a seasonal sight, evidence of a grandchild down for vacation. The median age of residents in the Parke Towers couldn't have been less than seventy-five. Even the doorman was pushing sixty.

Mrs. Steinmetz — "Lou, please" — let them into the apartment, expertly giving the room the once-over and flipping on the lights before stepping aside to let her clients enter.

Like the other apartments they'd been shown, this one looked transported from New York or Chicago or any other wintry Northern city. Little evidence of beach-living here. It wasn't so much the furniture, as Molly had thought at first, because on closer inspection she could see that the patterns actually were light and bright, a few colorful prints scattered around the place. The foreign sense here and in the other units they'd seen came from the old pictures on the walls, a treasured antique chair or desk or ottoman — frayed or scarred or fragile — given a place of honor in many of the rooms. Like at Pearl's, the rooms weren't so much living spaces as reminders of former rooms, galleries dedicated to the past. Tables in corners displayed family photos going back generations. Bar mitzvahs and weddings and vacations in the Catskills or Poconos. More recent shots, taken in Miami. Everywhere were pictures and albums and keepsakes. Notes and cards clung to every refrigerator: "I love grama," "To my zadie," all with love from Stacy or Sara or Jennifer or Jason or

Brandon or Jeffrey. And in every apartment, on one wall, one position of honor, a hand-tinted formal portrait of the couple who had left Russia or Poland or Germany to come to America.

Why not make a clean break with the past? Molly thought. Sweep it all away, clear it out and leave a lot of empty space, room for new stuff or just room to walk around. All this hoarding and storing. Molly couldn't distinguish one apartment from another. The only constant was Mrs. Steinmetz with her gravely voice that should have been accompanied by smoker's hack, only — "I haven't smoked in twenty-three years, you'll appreciate that, Doctor," smiling at Ben and placing her hand on his arm. Mrs. Steinmetz's — "Lou, please, 'Mrs.' makes me feel so old" — every movement was set to the music of her charm bracelet, the bulky chock-full kind Molly hadn't seen since she was a kid. It was loaded with a pearl-studded tennis racquet and a miniature golf bag and names set in hearts or discs. Mrs. Steinmetz had bleached hair, a shade somewhere between blond and pink, that hung artificially straight around her tanned face. From the back, because of her relatively slim figure, she could be mistaken for someone half her age. (Molly wasn't good at guessing, but this could be anywhere from mid-sixties to late seventies.)

Mrs. Steinmetz settled herself centrally in the living room — she had done this in every apartment — where she could keep an eye on Molly and the men, or "the boys," as she called them, and answer any questions. She seemed to have some second sight that told her exactly where Ben and Jerome were at all times. From her perch she would

169

call out, "Slide the master closet open." An obedient swoosh of rollers in their track would be followed by "She's right, Ben, look at this, cedar-lined." She'd done the same in each place, knew precisely which detail would catch their eye — custom jacuzzi tub, or dual shower heads, built-in shelving in a closet. Ben and Jerome wandered through the rooms, poking into cupboards and cabinets, and Mrs. Steinmetz guided them, unseeing but all-knowing, from her central location.

Molly crossed to the window and craned to see the patch of ocean visible between this building and the one across from it.

"Here, step outside."

Mrs. Steinmetz's rough voice so close startled Molly. Mrs. Steinmetz slid open the door to the terrace.

Molly leaned on the railing and looked out at the water. Mrs. Steinmetz had followed her — this was the first time she had abandoned her strategic position mid-unit — and stood slightly off to the side, like a car salesman allowing his customer to appreciate the vehicle before stepping in with his pitch.

"So," Mrs. Steinmetz began, "your father's moving to Miami. You must be very relieved."

Molly thought of all the emotions she might be feeling, and relief was not among them.

"It'll be so much better for him to be here with his family," Mrs. Steinmetz rasped.

"He's very busy with his practice."

Mrs. Steinmetz waved this away like cigarette smoke. "Sure, but he'll be busy down here too. Just not with work. Your father's still young, and he's so active. He'll love Miami. There's a lot for him to do. And his brother can show him around."

Molly thought of the two of them getting lost on the way back from the airport.

"It's good, at a certain point, to just be home again."

This has nothing to do with home, Molly fumed to herself. And what did Mrs. Steinmetz mean by "at a certain point"? What point? When you're too old to work? Ben wasn't like that.

"And this is a much better place than the city for him to entertain his first grandchild." Mrs. Steinmetz winked at her. "I think it's terrific. And it'll be so good for your father . . . he was telling me . . . Such a tragedy, your brother — such a promising young man — and then your mother." Mrs. Steinmetz shook her head. "They sounded like such wonderful people both of them. I know he's had a big loss, but I envy your father. It sounds like he had a good marriage, and however long you have that, you're lucky. My late husband — well, never mind." Mrs. Steinmetz wiped away his memory with her hand. "But your father is lucky."

Luckily at that moment Jerome joined them, expressing his enthusiasm for the place, listing its pluses in order, comparing this unit to the others they'd seen. Mrs. Steinmetz looked to Ben. He was the prospective buyer, after all.

"Nice," Ben said. "Very nice."

"Good." Lou smiled knowingly, already proficient at reading his code. "That means you like it. We'll keep it on the list."

• • • • •

The family gathered for a late lunch at Ruth's and said their goodbyes. Molly, not up for dealing with the whole truth, extended an open invitation to any or all of them to come visit her and Alix.

"And the baby!" Ruth chimed in, "We'll charter a plane for that!"

Molly smiled, she hoped convincingly. Hugs and kisses and lipstick smeared on cheeks and chins, and next thing she knew she was in the car with her father, Jerome at the wheel, heading for the airport.

Jerome dropped them at the curb. "Thank God you only turn seventy-five once," he said, handing Ben his suitcase. "I couldn't do this every year."

"Your party's next, buddy," Ben said.

"Oh no. I'm going to Paris. Find myself a date, hop on the Concorde, and I'm off."

Ben smiled. "I'll bring the Girls and we'll surprise you at the Eiffel Tower."

"Don't you dare." But Jerome smiled too. He said goodbye to Molly and hugged her. "Don't be a stranger."


Molly fished out her crossword puzzle book as soon as she'd strapped herself in. She worked the clues obsessively, hoping to drive thoughts of Alix out of her head. Impossible. After eight years she couldn't extricate Alix from even the most mundane observation.

"Your mother used to do those in ink," Ben said.

Molly jiggled her pen for her father to see.

"I never had the patience for them."

He had once threatened Claire: "Either the

crosswords or me." She had just looked at him. "Don't tempt me." But it was only a joke between them.

Her parents were Molly's one example of true love at first sight. At least on Ben's part. The night they met he'd said to Claire, "I'm going to marry you."

"What'd you say, Mommy?" This had been one of Molly's favorite stories.

"I just laughed," her mother always said. "Little did I know."

Molly wished for once that an important relationship in her life had a chance to play itself out, not be cut short by death. Or babies.

Ben slept for most of the flight, waking up for his meal, pressing his seat down before his tray had been cleared. Molly worked a puzzle or stared out the window. Three rows behind them a baby screamed nonstop.

# *Alix*

I don't like flying alone. I had looked forward to flying back home with Molly, though under the circumstances even if she had been with me it would have been like flying alone.

I couldn't even kiss her goodbye. I wanted to plaster my mouth to hers, my body to hers, all warm from sleep (what little either of us had gotten, and we both knew we were up but didn't or couldn't talk). I wanted to hurt her with my love the way she'd hurt me. Before I dried my hair, when she was watching me, I wanted to turn to her, wanted her to know I felt her eyes on me, wanted to feel that again, forever, wanted to go to her. But my body won't change her mind.

● ● ● ● ●

I called Carla even before I looked through the mail. I just left my bags in the middle of the living room and sat by the phone for a minute before dialing. I didn't want to think about it anymore, to try to figure out anything. I just wanted to *do*. And I didn't want anyone else's voice trying to change my mind.

I paced as I punched the numbers.

Carla's secretary put me right through. I've known Carla for fifteen years, but I had butterflies in my stomach when I heard her voice. My own voice came out shaky. "I'm ready to adopt."

Carla thought this was great news. "You and Molly want to come in today and start the paperwork rolling?"

"I just got off a plane from Miami. And Molly won't be coming in."

"It wouldn't be a problem. Dual adoption is not such a big deal anymore, at least not in California."

I said something else but Carla had me on her speakerphone. From my end she sounded like she was in a wind tunnel. Papers rustled. I heard her fax machine tocking away. I had to repeat myself. I spoke louder than I wanted to so Carla could hear me. "I said Molly's not going to do this with me." It was the first time I'd said it out loud. Not just telling someone but the volume of the telling made it more official. It knocked the air out of me and I stumbled to the couch.

The wind tunnel shut off when Carla picked up the handset. She sounded like she was right in the room with me. "What does that mean? Are you all right?"

"Can I come in tomorrow morning? I want to get started on this as soon as possible."

"No problem."

Easy for her to say.


Ben and Molly are probably in the city by now. I wonder if Molly and I were ever in the same place at the same time when we both lived in New York. Seems impossible for us not to have been. We've seen all the same movies and plays. We think we were at the same Bette Midler concert on two occasions, once in New York and then a few years later in L.A. I can't imagine being in a room with her and not being aware of her. Even now, angry and afraid as I am, three thousand miles away, I sense her presence.

# NEW YORK

# *Molly*

In the dark hallway outside his apartment Ben gave the bell his two short rings as he pulled out his keys.

He was just undoing the deadbolt when Jin called out from the other side. "Hallo, Doctor!" The door opened on her smiling face. "Come, come, doctor, come." She ushered Ben in, beaming at Molly.

"Hi, Jin," Molly said, hugging her.

"Molly . . . long time you no come." Jin seemed relieved Molly had arrived. She said no one else could get Ben to clear out some of the mess that had accumulated over the years.

Molly lugged her suitcase to her old bedroom. The furniture was the same she'd had in high school, so familiar she barely noticed it, and the shelves were still packed with books — all the Nancy Drew, a bunch of Black Stallions, as well as Signet editions of Austen, Dickens, George Eliot. Some of her college texts were mixed in also, plus books Ben had been given over the years. A few trophies from camp filled the gaps between volumes.

The dresser, empty of her presence for almost two decades, had become a repository for items Ben had moved off his own dresser — an antique set of glass perfume bottles that had been her mother's, and the silver brush, comb and mirror that belonged to her grandmother.

Over the years Molly had cleaned out all but one drawer. It still contained the odds and ends she couldn't bring herself to throw away but didn't need or want. A leather lens case for a Nikon she no longer owned, a set of shoelaces, unopened, about a foot of cloth labels with her name on them — she remembered her mother, a month or so before camp started, sewing them onto everything, shirts, shorts, socks, even the scratchy gray wool blanket emblazoned with the camp crest — an old envelope with color negatives the prints of which were God knew where. There was a change purse filled with Italian coins, a stack of *Playbill*s from past New York trips made with Alix or by herself.

The other five empty drawers provided ample room on Molly's visits, so she had let this one sit.

But Ben wanted her to go through everything and get rid of stuff. That was the word he had used on the plane.

"What 'stuff' exactly, Dad?" Molly asked.

"Just go through everything." (This from the guy who couldn't part with the daily paper. "I'm going to read those," he'd protest as Molly headed toward the garbage with a mound of old Sunday magazine sections. This happened each time she went home.)

"So this stuff you want me to go through, I can throw it out?"

"You don't have to throw anything out. Just put it in a pile. I'll go over it when I get home."

Molly fingered the lire in the change purse. Maybe this was the stuff he'd meant. She gathered the articles from the drawer. Dump the lens case? No, someone could use it. Same with the laces. The negatives and the labels, well they'd only mean something to her. She'd make a pile of things to bring back to L.A.

Ben had already started on some piles of his own. Mixed in with a bunch of art books stacked in the hall, Molly found an old Mills College catalogue from the '30s mixed in with the dusty volumes. The dated photographs and text would have amused her if she hadn't remembered her mother telling her that Mills had been her first choice but that she hadn't been allowed to go so far away for school. Claire hadn't made a big deal of it at the time, merely told the story and said Molly could go anywhere she wished.

Molly was still thumbing through the slick pages, yellowing only slightly at the edges, when Jin announced, "Molly, spring roll ready."

Jin had an extensive repertoire, but always, on Molly's first night in town, prepared a Chinese meal.

She served the spring rolls in the den. This used to be the playroom, but sometime after Michael died, after his room had been redecorated, the room was done over, the linoleum tile stripped, the hardwood floors scraped and polished. A new rug, clubby sofas, and built-in bookcases completed the look. Rechristened the den, it was a more serious room, befitting the more serious family they'd been forced to become.

"Look what I found," Molly said, holding up the catalogue for Ben.

"Where was that?"

"Mixed in with those art books."

Ben thumbed idly through it. "Did you apply here?"

"Dad, that's from Mommy. Mills was her first choice."

"But she went to Barnard."

"Because Grandma wouldn't let her go to school in California. She said it was too far away."

Ben put the catalogue down and started on another spring roll. "Your mother did very well at Barnard."

"Especially considering she didn't want to be there."

Ben and Molly ate dinner in the dining room. They didn't talk much. Mostly Ben listened as Jin told him what had happened while he was gone. No one had come to fix the dripping faucet in his bathroom. The butcher was supposed to deliver meat that afternoon but hadn't. She needed more money for groceries. Ben teased her, said he wouldn't give her more, she was too expensive. Jin teased right back — he wouldn't eat then.

When Molly was in L.A. this was how she pictured them — her father at the head of the table, talking to Jin while he ate, both of them alternately understanding and misunderstanding each other. Ruth had hired Jin after Claire died. She came from Hong Kong and had a sister who lived in Queens. She cooked, cleaned, did the marketing, watched Chinese shows on cable. She and Ben seemed as settled as a married couple.

As much as Molly would have liked Ben to find someone to be with — or, remembering how displeased she'd been by Louise Steinmetz's attention, as mixed as she felt about it — she couldn't really imagine him with anyone except Claire. She'd met all the women he'd dated over the years. Some she hadn't liked at all; some were okay. Molly had grown indifferent to them because that was how Ben seemed about them. And he always ended up back home with Jin.

"So, what are you going to do while you're here?" Ben asked her between bites.

"Sort and pack, remember?"

"Don't you want to see any shows?" he asked. One of his patients could get house seats to just about anything. Molly had grown up not buying retail and rarely going to the box office.

Her father was treating this trip like a vacation. Molly saw it as a horrible chore. It had already disrupted her relationship. She never would have said what she'd said to Alix if she hadn't been under such pressure about the apartment, even if that was what she had felt. Now it would take her months to heal the rift. She just wanted to get her job done here and get back to L.A. as fast as possible. But she'd already stirred up some ghosts with the Mills catalogue. A little distraction couldn't hurt.

"I might call Julia. And maybe Gloria." When they had been lovers, Gloria's exuberance sometimes grated. It would be a welcome distraction this trip.

After dinner Molly left Ben sorting through boxes and went to call her friends.

"I want to hear everything about everything," Gloria said. But Molly put her off till their dinner the next night and kept the conversation safely chatty, telling her friend about Ben's party, his move to Miami.

Molly had no trouble keeping her call to Julia, her best friend from high school, short. Julia's ten-year-old daughter needed help with her homework, so Julia excused herself after promising to rearrange her schedule so she could have lunch with Molly the next day. "Is Alix pregnant yet? I want you to catch me up on everything."

Molly's distractions were proving fraught with land mines. The whole evening had been like a weird mix of time zones, where her present life and different points in her past intersected. Surrounded by old possessions, in touch with old friends and lovers, Molly lost sight for a moment of what had changed. Except she hadn't called Alix, and Alix hadn't called her.

After she climbed into bed she lay awake a long time in the semi-dark. Faint light filtered around the edges of the window shades. Out on the street two guys fought or joked loudly. Trucks rattled up First Avenue, an occasional horn blared — hardly the sounds of the distant freeway she'd grown accustomed to. The city pounded right outside the walls, slipped in through the open window, curled up at the foot of her bed. No matter how many years Molly lived in California, coming to New York was coming home. No matter how many new buildings went up, or how many old stores closed and new ones opened, the city was as familiar to her as her own name.

Molly woke with that same heaviness she'd experienced the day before in Miami. The only thing she knew to do was to push herself into her tasks. By midmorning she had sorted through most of the contents of the bookcases and built-ins in the den. Sunlight streamed through the windows and the blank eyes of apartment buildings across the street watched her progress.

She could no longer walk across the room because she had piled books and records and magazines and games everywhere. Her original idea had been to have two piles — keep and question. She wanted to start packing — one of Ben's patients owned a moving company and had delivered a slew of cartons — but Ben would insist on going through everything himself. Molly took a deep breath and turned to tackle the last shelf.

A short stack of food magazines, several sample packets of outdated medicines — definite tosses — and a shirt box from Bergdorf Goodman. The last shirt box she'd opened, from Saks, had contained a set of silver nut dishes from Tiffany, three silver ashtrays monogrammed *R* and two silver Ronson table lighters that shot Molly back to parties her parents used to give, with the Lipton onion soup dip and tiny foil-wrapped cubes of Laughing Cow cheese as hors d'oeuvres.

She put one of the lighters on her L.A. pile, even though no one smoked anymore.

She'd already come across other items that tugged at memories she didn't know she had. Some of the objects, familiar though she hadn't seen them for years, enforced her sense of time warp. A tea cozy. A fondue pot. A Louis Sherry candy tin, purple decorated with a garland of violets and bright green leaves. How many had they had around the house? She'd used hers for her crayons. Michael's had held his coin collection. Apparently her mother had one, too. Molly opened it and tears stung her eyes. Its contents more familiar than memory, not thought of or remembered in years, but now, in front of her, so real she expected that if she called Michael or her mother to come see what she'd found they'd be at her side in a second. Michael's wallet. Brown leather worn dark and shiny from use. It contained his driver's license, his Red Cross Life Saver's card, eighteen dollars and a picture of a girl Molly hadn't thought about in years. Rattling around with the wallet were Michael's watch (frozen at 10:23), a Mustang key ring, and forty-three cents — a quarter, three nickels, three pennies, none dated later than 1966.

Molly pictured the wallet casually tossed on Michael's dresser along with loose change and keys and notes to himself. Or as a bulge in his back left pocket, where it left a dark outline on his chinos.

Cindy Fuller. That was the girl's name. Michael

had just started dating her that summer. Molly remembered her crying at the funeral.

A cloth-covered box held hankies, some very elaborate, finely embroidered, others plain. Molly sniffed one, smelling the memory of her mother. She put it in her pocket.

Now she tugged at the Bergdorf's box, almost afraid of what memory she'd drag down with it. It was surprisingly light and rattled a little when Molly lifted it off the shelf. She could only smile and shake her head when she opened it.

Fifty-six — she counted — of those tiny plastic cups Ben's pills came in when he was in the hospital. An absurd number of individually wrapped straws she didn't bother to count, but there were a handful. The ends of several cardiogram strips, the part the nurse tears off and throws away before giving the rest to the doctor. (Since no one would show him his results, Ben would scrounge these out of the wastebasket in an effort to keep abreast of his condition.) One plastic wrist ID bracelet, neatly cut so that Ben's name and number were legible.

Did he give equal weight to all this stuff? The plastic pill cups and the silver nut dishes? Michael's car keys and a bunch of paper straws?

She wanted to tell Alix about what she'd found. Many times she'd wanted to call Alix to ask, "Would we want..." whatever. Then she thought she'd better just leave Alix alone, not stir up anything. They could work everything out when she got home. But by now she'd rooted and sorted herself into a melancholy that only Alix could comfort, and Molly risked a rocky start to get to a real conversation.

She checked her watch. Eleven-thirty, eight-thirty in L.A. Alix would be up, breakfast finished, probably reading the paper.

All true, Molly ascertained from a terse Alix. The chill came through the wire. "Look," Molly said, "I want to apologize for what I said yesterday morning."

"I'm glad you finally got it out."

"Alix . . . really. I'm sorry. I'll make it up to you when I get back."

After a long icy silence Alix said, "I called Carla. She's helping me with the adoption."

Molly's knees buckled. She braced herself against a carton. "But we were going to talk."

"Talk about what, Molly? We've talked for three years. Or at least I have. This should not come as such a surprise."

"What about us?"

The longest silence yet. Molly heard the miles between them, the vast empty space of a continent before Alix responded. "It's your turn to tell me. You know what I want." Alix hung up.

All Molly heard was the light static of a dead line, then a recording telling her if she'd like to make a call, please hang up and dial again.

She stood in the middle of the room wanting to grab something — the Ronson had great heft — and hurl it through the window. Lob the marble fruit after it, followed by a flurry of cocktail napkins and guest towels, the fondue pot.

"What right —" she'd started to say, realizing Alix wouldn't hear anything she had to say. But what right did Alix have to do that when she knew, she knew, that Molly wasn't sure? Alix had gone on and on about her rights and her wants and her needs. For three years, Molly had listened to what Alix envisioned for them, what Alix saw in their future. *What about my needs?* Molly fumed.

She snapped open a thirty-three-gallon trash bag, blindly stuffed it with magazines and *Playbills* and brittle paperbacks, butterfly coasters and pink and orange cocktail napkins, a tea cozy and the straws and pill cups and cardiogram ends. She stomped her foot into the bag to pack everything down, to make room for the Mills catalogue, old cooking magazines, souvenir ashtrays, playing cards from Air France. She was sweating, panting before she stopped, realizing she'd dumped Ben's life when it was her own she wanted to clean out.

She sat on the edge of the couch, the only space available to her, and methodically pulled everything back out of the bag. When it was neatly restacked, more piles added to the jumble on the floor and coffee table, she threaded her way through the mess to shower and dress for lunch with Julia.

Getting out of the apartment provided some relief for Molly's claustrophobia. She wanted to walk up to the museum, stride, actually run full out to release some of her tension, but she was late so she took the First Avenue bus up to 81st Street and walked over to Fifth. Much to her surprise the city, the brownstones, helped. Sometimes when she read the *New York Times* between trips she'd suddenly cry when she came upon a totally innocuous picture, and then she'd know it was time to visit. Today, on a beautiful spring day, warm enough in just the sweater and blazer she'd brought for Miami, she wanted to live here again, couldn't imagine, especially under the circumstances, why she didn't.

"So, come on, the suspense is killing me." Julia hadn't even waited until they were seated. Twenty-nine years erased by her eager tone, her manner that of Molly's best friend from high school, not that of the first female vice president at the Metropolitan Museum. "Is Alix pregnant yet?"

Molly's resolve not to talk about it — because if she didn't talk about it, didn't give it credence, maybe it wouldn't be happening — lasted about twenty seconds in the face of Julia's concern. Out came the whole story, including the final chapter with that morning's phone call.

"Well, there's nothing wrong with adoption, you're not going to love the baby any less."

Molly had to explain that it wasn't where the baby came from but Baby, period.

"I couldn't imagine my life without my kids. I think you guys would be great parents, but it's so much work, you both have to really want it. What does Alix think?"

"She's made her choice. I lost."

Julia didn't push Molly to talk, didn't try to change her mind or convince her one way or another. She even let Molly change the subject to work and art and various shows making their way around the country.

Not until they'd ordered coffees did Julia drop her bombshell. "You know I hear things sometimes. Like, rumors about an upcoming vacancy in paintings conservation. Not that I've talked to anybody about it, or it's official or anything, but if it were something you'd be interested in I'd check into it for you."

Molly's first thought went to Alix. Would she be willing to move? But then, were she and Alix even going to be together? Molly's mind raced. *Forget the personal side for a moment, consider the work.* There'd be no more worrying during slow periods, no more crummy porcelain figurines, no more second-rate portraits. She'd have state-of-the-art facilities. Working on her own had lots of advantages, but paintings conservation at the Met...

"So?"

Molly looked up, startled.

"Want me to check into it?"

Molly just nodded and stirred her coffee.

She didn't stay to see any of the exhibits. Needing air and space, she headed straight for Central Park. On a dreary winter palette punctuated by buds, forsythia was just opening, bright yellow exclamations shooting into the otherwise drab scraggly branches.

Since she'd landed the day before, two themes had played, contrapuntal, in her head, present and past butting against each other. Everything in the apartment, everything she saw on the street, was so familiar. Even she and Julia went back over twenty years. This was continuity, something she didn't have in California. And the possibility of work here represented one neat joining, seamless and logical, inevitable, she thought. Alix believed everything happened for a reason. In the context of Julia's offer, Molly saw her trip in a whole new light. She wasn't meant to lose New York (she'd even had a flash of taking over Ben's apartment, converting the den into Alix's music room). All those years she'd spent working for what Alix wanted. Suddenly presented with a choice that involved only herself, Molly thought about Baby, which had never been her idea, and all the decisions that had radiated from that one — moving to the Valley, limiting vacations and working more, their lives focused on one goal that had never been Molly's to begin with. She remembered the Mills catalogue. Did she want to hold on to a dream so long after it had died, a reminder of what might have been? Molly had her answer to Alix. She would present Alix with a choice, a counter-ultimatum. If Alix chose L.A., well, maybe these last three years had been one long preparation for goodbye.

Very easy to say that to herself sitting on a park bench in the sun. Harder as she began to walk back through the park.

Spring in New York made her think about spring at the Valley house a year before, new green and iris opening, birds nesting. Sitting outside with Alix and the Sunday papers, everything seemed right with the world until she looked up and saw Alix crying.

"What's wrong?"

Alix just shook her head.

"Come on." Molly went to her, leaned over and wiped away some tears.

"What if this isn't meant to be?"

"Don't talk like that."

"But what if it isn't? I've tried everything, done everything they said, took everything they prescribed. I'm so scared that because I haven't gotten pregnant it means I'm not supposed to have a baby."

And Molly had once again been in the position of encouraging and sponsoring something she didn't want. Well, she wanted to ask now, what if it had meant Alix wasn't supposed to have a baby? What if it meant they were supposed to come to New York to start over?

Back and forth, back and forth, Molly's thoughts ran as she made her way across town and into the cool lobby of her father's building. Everything in the city was so familiar that she'd arrived before she realized she'd walked all the way home.

She put the Mills catalogue into her bag, a reminder to stay her course. She didn't do any more sorting that afternoon, just looked through old photo albums until it was time to meet Gloria for dinner.


Molly spotted Gloria waiting outside the restaurant. She hadn't changed in the fifteen years Molly had known her, except for a little gray starting to appear around her temples.

Molly hugged her, and Gloria spoke before they broke their grasp. "If you want, there's a really good program at the Kitchen."

"Never again," Molly said. Gloria had dragged her to more experimental films and videos than Molly could or wanted to remember.

"No, these are supposed to be really good."

"This trip is stressful enough," Molly said.

"Hard to think of giving up New York?" Gloria waited until they had settled into their booth before asking.

"There are some new developments." Molly filled Gloria in on the possible job, her possible move back to New York.

"This is so cool. I can introduce you and Alix to tons of women."

"I didn't say Alix was coming with me." Molly told Gloria about Baby, about Alix's call to Carla, the plans to adopt.

"You think Alix is going to leave you because you don't want a baby?"

Molly went numb at the thought expressed so directly. She just nodded.

"Did she say that?"

"She didn't have to."

"She'll never leave. You guys have been together forever."

"Eight years isn't forever."

"For some lesbians it is." Gloria sipped her wine. "You'll work this out."

"I've never seen her so set on anything before."

"Maybe you're just looking for a way out."

Molly bristled at the idea.

"I don't mean that in a bad way," Gloria added. "Look, I've just gotten my life the way I like it. Work's good. I can travel when I want. I'm not the least bit interested in having kids."

"Since when?" Molly asked. "You used to talk about it all the time when we were together."

"Only because I thought you wanted one. Now, forget it. I don't even pretend." She sipped her wine.

"And it doesn't make me any less nice. I don't mind spending time with them. I just don't want one around on a permanent basis. Whatever happened to all the lesbians who weren't interested in having babies, anyway?"

Molly had wondered the same thing herself.

"I've got just the thing to cheer you up," Gloria said.

"I'm not interested."

"Molly, you don't even know what it is yet."

"You're going to take me to some hot new club so I can watch while you hit on women."

"God forbid you should have a good time, forget your troubles for a few hours."

Molly knew that she didn't envy Gloria's sex life, despite some pretty interesting tales over dinner — forays into the lighter side of S&M, the infinite possibilities of microwaveable Saran Wrap over the restrictions of dental dams. ("I mean, hell, Molly, a dental dam's only yea big." Gloria had spread her fingers to indicate the approximate size. "And Saran Wrap, well it comes in 200 foot rolls.") Molly didn't expect Gloria to understand the thrilling aspect of making love with the same person over the years, having Alix be so familiar and strange at the same time. Molly declined the invitation.

They hugged outside the restaurant, then each hailed a cab.

Molly gave her father's address to the driver. As they took off behind Gloria's cab, she thought of the apartment, the piles of stuff and half-filled boxes and the memories and disappointments. She thought of calling Alix, of not calling Alix. Alix wanted her to think. About what? Baby? The Mills catalogue pages flipped through her memory. Fuck it, she'd let Alix do some thinking.

Molly leaned forward and pointed at Gloria's taxi. "Driver, follow that cab."

At first glance Molly felt she'd fit in better at a straight bar. She wished Alix were next to her for support, encouragement. But then across the crowded dance floor, Molly spotted a woman who stood out from all the tattoos and piercings and hairstyles that made a statement. Hair pulled back off her face and gathered in a loose pony tail, she was dressed in black suede pants and an incredible blue shirt, royal blue Doc Martens. A total look that came apart if you cared to dissect it, but the package was so perfect, so why bother.

Of course Gloria knew her and introduced them. "Molly, Ariana. Ariana, Molly." Ariana was loosely with a group of four or five women who worked the room, circulating between the bar and the dance floor.

Ariana was reticent about what she did for a living. "Something with foundations, very boring. I try so hard to leave my job at the office. Don't you?" Ariana went to dance with one of her friends. Very expert at hip-hop, she looked just like a music video. Even sweaty she was attractive.

"Pretty hot, huh," Gloria said directly into Molly's ear, the only way to hear in the place.

"I'm a married woman," Molly yelled back.

"So you can't look?"

"Not my type," Molly said. She ordered a Glenlivet.

"I don't limit myself to one type. You gotta get out more."

"I wouldn't even remember what to do."

"It's like riding a bicycle. You can't forget." Gloria sipped her drink and scanned the crowd. She tapped Molly's shoulder and pointed to a tall, dark-haired woman working her way across the room toward them. "My date just arrived. Be still, my heart."

Gloria greeted her friend and steered her to Molly's spot at the bar. Lucinda was gorgeous. Gloria, unwilling to share her with anyone, took her immediately to dance. Molly wasn't alone for long, however. Ariana, taking a breather, reached across her to the bar for a napkin to wipe her face and neck. Ariana wore men's cologne. Molly liked that. The aroma was brisk and spicy, so unfamiliar it became exotic. Unlike the floral mysteries evoked by so many women's fragrances, this lively citrus made Molly take an extra breath each time it struck her nostrils.

"You like to dance?" Ariana asked.

"I don't get out much." Molly thought of her episode with Alix on the dance floor.

"I didn't think I'd seen you around."

"I live in L.A."

"Cool. I love L.A. The clubs there are great. You ever go to Girl Bar? Klub Banshee?"

Ariana knew a different city from the one Molly lived in. Dance clubs and sex clubs and pool parties. Ariana's eyes were blue, Molly realized, like her shirt — she'd almost missed their color in the dim light. And although she talked to Molly, Ariana didn't miss a trick, waving to other women, patting those she knew as they walked by. She drank Bacardi and soda because it was "surprisingly refreshing." Every so often she wiped her fingers over the sweating glass and then traced the moisture across her forehead, down her neck, under her ponytail. All the while she kept talking to Molly, asking questions about nothing important — "How do you know Gloria?" "How long have you lived in L.A.?" — nothing intimate, nothing personal, but constant and punctuated by her attempts to cool herself off, fingers feathering her face, neck, dipping down the V of her shirt.

No one had flirted with Molly in so long that she didn't pick up on it at first. A light touch on the arm, a smile or a wink, and that constant movement of Ariana's hand over her face, down her neck, pulling her blouse away from her body to let air circulate.

Molly was flattered by the attention and responded automatically. Like riding a bicycle. Gloria and Lucinda had joined them, and they were having a dishy conversation about movie stars. Gloria would say something and Ariana would agree, turning slightly to Molly for confirmation. Molly was pleased when Ariana noticed her.

She couldn't keep her eyes off Ariana's blouse. It was perfect. A flowing silk or rayon, bright deep blue, it had smooth blue oval buttons that beckoned her. Molly wasn't accustomed to undressing women with her eyes but she kept slipping those buttons through their holes.

She didn't go further than that. She didn't imagine the body underneath its softness. Just that tantalizing vision of Ariana standing before her, that blue blouse hanging open.

Ariana sprang to her feet. "This is my favorite song." She grabbed Molly's hand. Molly didn't have time to protest. " 'Scuse us, Glo."

When they stepped onto the dance floor Ariana flung her arms around Molly's neck, effectively thrusting her pelvis into Molly's. Molly's hands landed on Ariana's ribcage. Ariana linked her hands behind Molly's head, then leaned back and closed her eyes, smiling and swaying to the music. Molly saw the vulnerable neck, all the smooth places Ariana had dabbed at to cool herself off.

Accustomed to dancing with Alix, and then only rarely, Molly hesitated, unsure what to do. But Ariana's dancing dictated not only the rhythm of her feet but the placement of Molly's hands. She felt the curves of Ariana's body, the planes of her back, the taut skin over her ribs.

In the meantime, Ariana's hands had ventured into the soft folds of Molly's shirt.

Molly felt Ariana's fingers playing in the ripples,

gathering up the material, smoothing it, thumbs measuring distances, hands dipping dangerously low, lightly, dusting Molly's back with her fingers. Molly closed her eyes for one second and saw a clear picture of smooth skin.

A warning bell sounded in her head. Ariana had inched closer. This was no longer an innocent dance. Molly's own hands had become greedy, smoothing away material to grope for the solid substance underneath. She and Ariana had shifted imperceptibly so that instead of being head on, thigh to thigh, they were off-center, thighs between legs, rocking slowly, keeping time.

Molly remembered this part of bicycling only too well. "I need another drink," she said, though it was the last thing she needed.

"I'll get you one," said Ariana, leading her by the hand back to their seats. She didn't sit though, simply grabbed both their jackets off the backs of the chairs, told Gloria they were leaving, and pulled Molly out of the bar onto the street.

A slight drizzle fell. Molly looked up into a streetlight and saw hundreds of misty drops bouncing, hovering, seemingly not falling. Ariana had let go of her hand to put on her jacket.

"Here," Ariana said, laying Molly's jacket across her shoulders. "I live just a few blocks away."

"Oh, no, I've got to . . ." But Molly didn't know what she had to do.

"Come on," said Ariana. "I owe you a drink."

The drizzle graduated into a soft steady rain. It didn't rain like this in California. Or if it did, Molly was always driving somewhere, never got a chance to enjoy it. She missed this, missed New York. How could she have left it? A gay couple walking arm-in-arm stopped, kissed passionately, continued on.

"In here." Ariana's tug made Molly aware that they'd been holding hands since they started walking.

Ariana's apartment was at the top of two steep flights of narrow stairs. Molly heard herself panting as she waited for Ariana to unlock the door. "I really think I should —" but before she could say "be going," Ariana had yanked her inside.

The living room was done in '50s furniture, turquoise and pinto and molded plastic. Neo retro something. A definite look but nothing comfortable. Molly had seen that before, but she had never seen such a collection of games and magazines outside a museum or display case. Everywhere were board games — Monopoly, Parcheesi, several versions of Scrabble, Chinese checkers — and stacks of *Life* and *Look*. A couple of *Time* magazines neatly displayed on the curved coffee table were dated 1959.

Ariana, obviously accustomed to guests pausing on the threshold, went about the room straightening up, checking her answering machine, getting glasses and ice. "Come on into the kitchen, this room's not really for sitting."

Molly could have sworn Ariana had said something after that, and followed her into the kitchen to ask.

"Are you sticking with Scotch, or do you want something else. Cognac?" Ariana asked. "Wait, I've got Glenlivet. Better not to mix drinks."

This room was as kitschy as the other, though perhaps not as true to one era. Here the decades slammed into each other, Howdy Doody met Pee-wee Herman. This crazy room was chock full of collectibles: salt shakers in the shapes of coconuts hanging from a palm tree, airplanes, Carmen Miranda cows. The cookie jar was a white rabbit, its ears convenient handles, the clock a platter of eggs sunnyside up, minutes and hours marked by strips of bacon. There were mugs with protruding dog heads, a cow pitcher for milk. Some daffodils — these at least seemed real — stood in a ceramic paper bag vase.

A huge birdcage dominated one corner of the room. From it came what Molly had thought was Ariana's voice. "Hi, Gwen. Let me out. Billy wants out."

Molly stared at the two birds.

"That's Billy, the green one," Ariana said as she pulled bottles from a cupboard. "He's a Yellow Nape. The other's an African Gray. Billy's the talker, aren't you, Billy?"

The parrot strutted on its roost. The other bird, gray with a red tail, eyed Molly. Billy spoke again. "Hi, Gwen. Let me out."

Molly asked, "Who's Gwen?"

"Me," said Ariana. "I was born Gwen Doak. Who would you rather be, Gwen Doak or Ariana Cassini? I had it legally changed a year ago. Billy sticks with Gwen."

Molly sat at the table — the kind of huge wooden spool that she had seen at construction sites all over the city — while Ariana poured Glenlivet into two rocks glasses.

"Gee, where'd you get those?" Molly asked, surprised to see something so ordinary. The phone rang but Ariana made no move to answer it. "Don't you want to get it?"

"It wasn't the phone. It was Patty." Ariana pointed to the gray bird with the red tail.

"She sounded exactly like the phone. How can you tell them apart?"

"The parrot only rings twice."

"Good title for a book," Molly said.

Ariana didn't react.

Exhausted, Molly sat in this strange kitchen with this incredibly attractive woman who had come on to her. She didn't want the drink. She didn't even really want Ariana. (And even if she did, she would be afraid to see what her bedroom looked like.)

Molly knew she didn't belong here. She ached for something familiar, despaired of finding it any-where — in this room, in her father's jumbled apartment. Even if she were in L.A., what would be familiar at this point?

"I should get going."

"You haven't taken a sip."

"Sorry."

"I thought maybe you'd like to stay for a while." As Ariana talked she pulled her hair out of her ponytail and shook it over her shoulders. Killer gesture, just like in the movies. Molly wanted to fall for it. Ariana stood over her, untucked her blouse — exactly what Molly had yearned for since she first spotted her across the bar — leaned down and kissed Molly on the lips. "Come on," she whispered as she started to unbutton her beautiful blue blouse. "We could go right to bed."

Molly placed her hands on Ariana's wrists to stop their action. "I can't." She disentangled herself, stood up. "I'll find my way out." Molly left Ariana standing there, shirt open just as she had imagined it. As she walked right out of her own fantasy the phone rang again. Or maybe it was the parrot.

Molly stood in the den, surrounded by boxes and piles of stuff — really the most appropriate word for the assortment of objects she'd been trying to classify for her father's inspection. Stacks of books and old suitcases, a projector and a hundred unlabeled boxes of slides, mixing bowls and kitchen utensils that hadn't been used for years, trays of brandy snifters and sherry glasses, piles of linens and towels, records — both 78s and 33s.

A set of her grandfather's books on Chinese porcelain she had set aside for herself. But what about everything else? Vases and cachepots and candlestick holders and a multitude of serving dishes and platters and more copper cookware than Julia Child would know what to do with. A mass of things overwhelmed the usually ample space in the apartment.

Molly had decided to keep very little of what she'd found. None of it really reflected the lives that had been lived here. Strewn about this way — napkins and tablecloths left lying on top of the sideboard and dining table, seldom-used pots and pans hauled out of the kitchen and left in the middle of the living room — everything looked sad and out of context. The shelves looked more than empty. Without their usual contents Molly could see how they sagged in places, needing a paint job. The whole apartment looked a little grubby, a little neglected, already abandoned.

Ben had taken the day off to begin his own sorting. She checked on his progress. He'd started on his closet and had pulled out most of his clothes. His room looked like his closet had exploded, suits and sports jackets and ties and shoes and sweaters strewn everywhere.

"Now what?" Molly asked in amazement. The sheer volume amazed her. She'd never thought of her father as a clothes horse.

"How much of this will I wear in Miami? Look, I must have two hundred ties."

He had laid them out on the bed — stripes and paisleys and solids and florals — and had draped some around his neck, others hung from his arms. Molly picked up one with a linked chain pattern, the background a particularly vivid orange. "Dad, this is really ugly."

"But it's Hermes. Very expensive."

"Dad, it's really ugly. Have you ever worn it?"

Ben reluctantly put the tie on a pile that Molly hoped was for charity. "What time's your flight?"

"Seven-thirty. I'll be able to get a lot of stuff packed if you can tell me what you want and what you don't want."

"I have no idea where to begin."

"You'll get the hang of it. But you have to be ruthless. Remember, you'll be moving into a smaller apartment."

"But there'll be an extra room for you and Alix and the baby."

"Swell, Dad." She dumped another tie — silver and black, strictly Mafia — onto the charity pile, avoiding the topic of Baby. She passed her hands over the mound of ties, fingers nimbly digging through them for treasures or scrap. "Remember how you used to scrape the soles of my new shoes?"

Molly associated only the smallest rituals with her father. He had never presided over weekly Sunday dinners or made regular holiday speeches. Nothing even on her birthday, other than a kiss — or more likely an offered cheek and a finger pointed right to it. "It's your birthday, give me a kiss."

But they had observed certain family practices when she was young. Like whenever she bought a new pair of shoes, leather soles smooth as mirrors, she would bring them to Ben when he came home, not to show them off, for though he might comment on how pretty they were, he never seemed too interested in the style, more in the potential danger of those slick soles. And he would take his key and score deep lines in each, roughing them up so Molly wouldn't slip.

"Whatever made you think of that?"

"I don't know." Who knew anymore why a strobing electric blue-and-yellow striped tie triggered a totally unrelated memory. These past few days her neurons fired at will, hit the oddest targets.

"So," Ben said.

"So," Molly repeated, never knowing with her father if she was supposed to continue a conversation or wait for a question.

"What's happening with Alix? Am I any closer to being a grandfather?"

Molly had deliberately not responded to his hint about the extra room, had been avoiding this discussion since she landed in Miami. Now that it sat between them, she didn't know what to say. She began cautiously. "Well, there's a new development. I had dinner with Julia last night."

"What's she up to?"

"The same," Molly said, "still at the museum." She fiddled with a Giorgio Armani, the first tie she liked. "That's the development. She said something about a job opening up in paintings conservation. Said if I was interested, I could probably get it."

"Why would you want to come back here?"

Molly opened her mouth to answer but no sound came out, blocked by the light drizzle that had fallen as she and Ariana left the bar, the cab ride home, sailing through the dark streets of the city, meter clicking, a talk show on the radio playing so softly she couldn't make out the words. So familiar, all of it, every block and every building, so comfortable and so right. She imagined her father's apartment vacant. Or worse, inhabited by strangers.

"It's nothing definite. Just a possibility." She grabbed a cluster of rep ties and added them to the giveaway pile.

"Sure you want to raise a child here?"

"What's so bad about that? I liked it," Molly said.

"What does Alix think?"

"She's very supportive of my work." Coward, Molly thought. So this too would end up like every other revelation she'd made to her father. On the run, the last thing before they got off the phone — *Oh, by the way, the baby with Alix, not going to happen, probably end the relationship too, talk to you next week.*

She spent the next hours packing and helping Ben decide what treasures to take with him to his new life. She'd ordered a car from one of the Israeli services the night before. They were cheaper than cabs to the airport and the drivers didn't talk to you the way New York cabbies tended to. Molly wanted a quiet ride to Kennedy. She arranged for it to come early, allowed for rush hour and gave herself extra leeway on top of that. She wanted the least amount of time in the apartment, preferring to wait at the airport than have to look around at what she might never see again.

She packed boxes until the last minute, when the doorman buzzed to announce that the car had arrived. She hurried to zip her suitcase, careful not to look around her room. She had no language for how to leave it.

She'd managed to accomplish a lot, and the apartment had a new order, boxes filled for Miami, some for charity. Not very neat, but purposeful at least, stuff no longer lying in useless piles. After a tearful goodbye to Jin, promising to write, thanking her for taking such good care of her father, Molly went downstairs with Ben.

She took a deep breath in the elevator. "Did that," she said.

"Yup." Ben picked up her suitcase and held the door.

The double-storied lobby had dark wood paneling, slate floors polished to a high sheen, and mullioned windows, some with stained glass panes. The slate tiles were varying sizes, squares and rectangles, in multiple shades of gray. Molly and Michael used to see how fast they could get from the entrance to the elevator without stepping on the lines between the tiles. Molly still tore down the hall when the doorman wasn't around.

How did she do something like this for the last time? She knew she'd be back in a few weeks to interview for the museum job, that her father probably wouldn't have found a place in Miami by then, but the plans were made, the changes already in motion. Each step she took moved her closer to a new future, a new arrangement of the blocks that comprised her life.

The lobby became a gauntlet she walked through, her past on either side of her. It flooded her with sharp memories that went way beyond the slated halls of the building: Schraft ice cream sandwiches from the bakery; the Busy Bee Market, gone for years, and its owner Manny, who ordered Wonder Bread for Claire because Molly insisted on the red yellow and blue balloons just like she was told to on TV; the time she fell and bit her tongue, tears and blood pouring off her face, Claire dressed up, a handkerchief on her shoulder, carrying a screaming Molly down the block — screaming but, in memory at least, safe in her mother's arms.

Out in the warm spring air Ben offered his cheek for a kiss. Molly hugged him.

"Have a safe flight," Ben said.

"I love you, Daddy."

"Me too, Molly."

As Molly settled into the seat she looked back at her father on the curb. He waved at her, then turned his fingers toward his face, pointing out the tracks of imaginary tears.

The car radio sputtered information in both Hebrew and heavily accented English. Pickup at 49th and Madison at six forty-five. Pickup at La Guardia for delivery to Upper West Side, Riverside and 86th, who's taking it? With each garbled transmission Molly pictured the neighborhoods, down to the quality of the light, the type of buildings, brownstones or shop fronts.

She kept telling herself she'd be back soon, but the thought of what waited for her in L.A. made her wish she could just stay now, slip back into life here as if she'd never left.

"Which airline, please?" the driver asked.

"American."

Just over the Triborough Bridge Molly turned back to see her city. How familiar, she thought again, how home. The silver-skinned Citicorp building pinpointed her neighborhood. Its slanted roof guided her eye. Since it had been built she knew exactly where her street was, with no need to approximate as she had before — a little to the right of the Chrysler Building and the Waldorf Towers. She could look from this distance, or see a photograph, and imagine what was going on below the skyline. The gridlock at Third and 54th, the heat rising from the vents above the Lexington Avenue subway, the fruit stand in front of the post office. She might not remember each brick or even each store or restaurant, but the feel, the sensations of the area were palpable, something she breathed in and never exhaled. She saw interiors also: Ariana's mixed-up kitchen, Ben's bright kitchen, fruit ripening on the counter, Jin's wok at the ready.

She closed her eyes to see more, but a different movie ran on the back of her lids: Alix cursing over the ironing board, playing her violin under the huge shade tree on the front lawn one summer day, walking along the beach with the dog.

Molly brought all this with her as she flew across the country. A jumble of images perfectly reproduced but incomprehensible to her, as if she had become a camera, able to record with precision and accuracy everything around her but with no resource for interpretation.

# CALIFORNIA

# *Alix*

I didn't have to take this session, but I didn't want to be home when she arrived. I'm not concentrating, which is bad because the music is tricky and the fingering difficult and I have to work hard at it. I'd hoped the job would take my mind off Molly's plane hurtling west at six hundred miles an hour, but my thoughts cover as much ground and about as fast.

Carla's started the process of finding a baby for me. She told me to tell everyone I know that I'm interested in adopting. If we're lucky, she said, someone I know will be able to help us. I had to give her biographical information: name, age, religion, education, yearly income, did I plan to work after the baby came.

"This could take a long time," Carla said, "so

stay busy." She hesitated a moment then said, "And work on Molly."

I just laughed at that. Imagined two goons taking Molly by the arms while a third threatened her with — but that's about as far as I got. Though if I had thought it would make a difference I'd have looked into hiring someone to do just that.

Carla came around her desk to hug me goodbye. I leaned against her for a moment. "Don't worry," she said. "Try to relax."

Impossible. I hold myself so tightly that my head doesn't really rest on the pillow at night; I have to consciously let it sink down, make sure I can feel the mattress supporting my body. I'm all knots and my head aches constantly.

Much to my surprise I called my mother when I got home from seeing Carla and told her everything. On the phone, spontaneously, without any buildup or warning. It was just the opposite of what I'd planned ever since the first insemination. I'd always envisioned making a special trip up there, just me, and working around to it gradually after spending a lot of time just talking about whatever — her neighbors, her vegetable garden, her volunteer work. Then I'd sidle around to my baby pictures, the scrapbook she'd compiled when I was young, containing locks of my hair, report cards, cute things I'd said. And when she asked why the sudden interest I'd say, very slowly, carefully, maybe even protecting my stomach (because I'd imagined myself pregnant for this, not one second before, and probably a few months along for safety's sake), "Because I'm going to have a baby."

I certainly hadn't expected to burst into tears

when my mother asked, "You sound a little blue, hon, something wrong?"

That was my real mother, the kind one, the one I remembered from growing up, chocolate chip cookies and unconditional love, before icebergs and breast cancer and years of chill and partial thaw and uneasy peace, always something stuck beneath a few surface layers.

When she asked what was wrong I cried like a baby, brokenhearted, inconsolable. I couldn't get out any words, so relieved to hear her old tone again. Whether I was right or wrong didn't matter to her, I was her daughter. Tears and words poured out of me then, everything at once, about Baby, and Molly's leaving me because of Baby, and my years of wanting and trying and not getting pregnant and the strain on the relationship, on both of us.

First my mother let me cry. Then she soothed me, comforted me. And before I even had enough breath to tell her about what Carla was doing my mother said, "Have you considered adoption?"

She didn't talk to me about Molly, except to say that raising a child is a huge responsibility and I'm better off knowing now if Molly doesn't want to undertake it.

She has called me every day, sometimes more than once. She even said she'd spread the word in Oregon because "You never know, dear." I finally asked her what had changed, why she was suddenly so accepting.

"It was just time, I guess."

I think it was more than that. Time may have melted every trace of ice, left her with the incontrovertible fact that I am her daughter and she loves me unconditionally, but I think Baby brought her back. Baby is driving Molly away but brought my mother back.

I'd be happy except for this hole in my heart and the dread of what's going to happen when Molly comes home. I want to feel safe with my mother on my side again but I can't because now Molly's out of reach.

I feel like I'm trying to stuff a huge pillow into a tiny box: as soon as one end is in and set, the other bulges out.

# *Molly*

When she finally got her luggage it was almost
2:00 A.M. New York time. Exhausted, not simply
from the trip but from her anticipation of dealing
with Alix, she shouldered her bags — the one she'd
brought for Miami and the extra one she'd filled at
her father's apartment — and waited outside the
terminal for a shuttle van to her end of the Valley.
Luckily she was the only passenger and they sped
along the empty dark freeway in silence.

When it dropped her off at her gate the dog
greeted her enthusiastically. Alix's car was gone. She
had left a note on top of the neat stack of mail on
the kitchen counter: "Double session, home very
late." Nothing about waiting up or not waiting up.
Nothing about welcome home. Nothing about love.

Molly gave Annie a dog biscuit, dumped her bags

in the bedroom, then, exhausted but keyed up, paced the house, room by room, trying to find some clue to belonging. Evidence was everywhere, books and CDs, photos of her, of Alix, of them together, with friends. Evidence too in the dog sticking by her side, glad to have her home. But what did *home* mean anymore? It had disappeared so easily when she was in New York.

Half-hoping Alix would walk in so she could get this over with, she stalled as long as she could, opening her mail, thumbing through the magazines that had arrived. She even took a quick hot shower to wash off the stale plane smells. But the house stayed empty so she crawled between clean sheets.

For all her bravado about wanting to face this, Molly pretended to be asleep when Alix came home. Alix eventually got into bed, careful to occupy only one tiny sliver of the queen-size mattress. Molly didn't curl around her, sneak a hand out to touch her, didn't infringe past the imaginary yet palpable boundary that had grown between them since Miami.


The dog didn't wake her to be let out so Molly slept until nine. An unusual stillness pervaded the house, explained by a note on the kitchen table: "8:45 — took Annie to the beach. A." Alix had left the coffee on, so Molly poured herself a cup, prepared to settle in with the paper. She sat at the kitchen table and stared out at the yard. The bearded iris looked about ready to pop. The Trinidad flame bush had lots of bristly red blooms, and the fuchsia bougainvillea sprung wildly from the back fence. The intermittent screeches of a red-tailed hawk played counterpoint to the constant rush of the freeway that echoed up their hill. For the first time since Julia's mention of the job, Molly thought about what it would mean to give up her studio, the kind of retreat you don't find in Manhattan. But then she remembered the Mills catalogue and reminded herself of what she might be giving up by staying. Under any other circumstances she could talk to Alix about this. She'd ask for a year. Let's just try it, she'd say. But now, driven by Baby, Alix had only one response to anything Molly brought up. She'd already given it, actually, by calling Carla. Her singleminded purpose excluded everyone else. Well, now it was Molly's turn to want something.

She changed into sweats and sneakers and drove to meet Alix.


Topanga Canyon cut through the Santa Monica Mountains to the Pacific. Tract homes on the Valley side gave way to ranches and funky cabins, vistas of rolling hills and meadows, then a little village, a hidden '60s subculture. Past that, the mountains took over again, breathtaking gorges and cliffs, groves of sycamore along a stream that became a torrent during the winter rains.

Molly loved this drive, the progression of neighborhoods and then the wilderness, giving way again on the beach side to houses. The change in the air, from warm Valley to cooler ocean, was noticeable miles before you reached Pacific Coast Highway. As much as she dreaded what she had to tell Alix, the drive calmed her a bit. She hadn't realized how much she'd missed this until she saw the green gorges. Topanga dropped right into the Pacific. If she didn't stop at PCH she could drive straight into the unusually calm blue-gray surf. At the first glimpse of the ocean her heart twinged a little, a little pang at the thought of giving this up.

She parked next to Alix's Volvo (bought for its safety record, best for Baby; the company even made its own baby seats) and walked down the flight of steps to the beach. She shaded her eyes with her hand to look for Alix and Annie. To her right first, past the lifeguard station in the direction of a stretch of houses built right on the sand. No sign of them. She turned toward her left, in the direction of Santa Monica. No houses down here, but a restaurant perched above some rocks at the far end.

She spotted them then, maybe half a mile up the beach, heading away from her, toward the rocks that jutted out into the water. The golden retriever trotted happily off the leash, sniffed at piles of kelp and driftwood, teased the waves. Old routine: walk the beach, sit by the rocks, then back the other way, maybe past the houses. Molly took a gulp of air for courage and called out to Alix who was too far away to hear but who turned anyway, as if she sensed Molly's presence, and waved back.

Alix broke into an easy lope and the dog ran alongside her. Alix gradually increased her pace, the dog keeping up until she decided to just go all out, and galloped ahead of Alix.

Alix slowed, hands on her hips. Even from the distance between them Molly could see she was gasping for breath.

Molly walked toward her, feeling again as if each step were taking her inexorably into the next stage of her life, narrowing her options. Poised on the brink of the narrowest part of an hourglass, she was one conversation away from being shot through to the other side. Amnesia would serve her well here, and Molly forced herself to focus on the future.

Alix picked up a piece of driftwood which she brandished over her head to get Annie's attention. The dog ran to her, jumping eagerly for the stick. Alix hurled it into the water and Annie went after it, swimming out for it and dropping it back at Alix's feet.

"Be careful, Alix, the current," Molly shouted into the wind. If Alix heard her, she didn't acknowledge it. This annoyed Molly. Just like Alix to let the dog go too far, never drawing the line between adventure and danger.

Molly remembered when they bought Annie. Eight weeks old, a furry blond bundle, the cutest puppy anyone had ever seen. A few nights after they brought her home, they'd had to leave her alone, barricaded in the kitchen. They'd filled the space with newspaper and toys, left water for her. When they came back three hours later the room was a wreck, papers and shit and water splashed everywhere. And in the middle of it all was Annie, lost and bewildered, tear streaks around her eyes. Had she been human, her face would have been puffy. Molly couldn't get the picture out of her head for weeks, and that sweet and vulnerable image of Annie had stayed with her all these years, made her want to protect the animal.

She'd been successful so far, perhaps her only success at protection — here she was, losing Alix. Not her first loss. But had she possessed any protective powers at age eleven? What if she had been in the car with Michael? Would she have died also? Or would Michael have been saved? Would those altered circumstances have been enough to shunt everyone's life onto a different track? Did she have any power to effect any kind of change?

She winced at the pain that Michael had become, any barrier to it shorn away in New York when she had found his wallet, stared at old pictures, remembered everything she'd spent years trying to forget.

Flooded with memory, amnesia impossible, she could access every detail of her life with Alix, every walk they had ever taken, every time they'd made love, fought, been bored together, restless, content. Their soundtrack punctuated by the cries of the red-tailed hawk, the braying crows, the owls in the smooth-trunked eucalyptus, backed up by the rhythmic summer chant of crickets, a monotonous two-count beat that now became a steady pumping: *Stay home, stay home, stay home.*

But where was that? Molly tried inserting a New York reel but those images had left her and she saw only the scene in front of her: the broad beach and Alix watching the dog.

Alix called Annie to her. Molly watched the dog scamper and dart and tease, kicking up sand, rolling in it out of sheer joy.

Why couldn't this have been enough for Alix?

A hundred yards separated them, but the distance seemed insurmountable. *Get this over with.*

Annie had stopped at attention to watch a flock of gulls lolling on the beach. Her hind leg quivered in anticipation as she stalked closer, slowly, slowly, until boom! she took off across the sand toward the patch of birds, running full out. Alix's encouraging cry — "Go, Annie" — floated back to Molly, distinguished from the whines of the gulls as they scattered, flying low out over the ocean, Annie in hot pursuit. She didn't stop until she stood in water to her belly.

Molly moved toward Alix just as the next set of waves built. She saw the dog standing in the roiling water. She knew what would come next. She yelled, "Alix, stop her."

Of course Alix couldn't hear her over the surf and the gulls and her own cheering. A wave swelled, water pulled back, down to Annie's paws now, and she stood proud in the undertow, looking to Alix for approval as the new set rose out of the old, looped back and crested to break down hard on the dog, who tumbled once, twice. Molly didn't see more because she was running now, running toward when everything she'd learned had taught her to run away, run from, anything not to lose again.

She grabbed Alix's sleeve. "How could you let her do that?"

"She's fine," Alix said. "Look."

Annie trotted out of the water, shook herself off, and ran down the beach to continue her explorations.

Molly looked from Annie to Alix, ready to scold

227

them both, out of her own fear and relief. Instead, she threw her arms around Alix with such force they both staggered for balance.

"What?" Alix asked, stroking Molly's back. "What?"

Without releasing her grip Molly let out a gasp of air. She felt like she'd spent years holding her breath, or whispering, never allowing herself full feeling of anything.

It wasn't that she didn't want a baby. She was afraid of losing a baby. How could she protect it from anything? From little hurts and disappointments — the broken toy, the pet that dies, the friend who moves away — to the big things, the final ones: the drunk driver, the showing off for a friend that leads to tragedy. Would scraping the soles of its new shoes make any difference in the world? How could she promise Alix everything would be all right? All she'd learned so far was that you can't protect those you love. Claire couldn't protect Michael, Ben couldn't protect Claire. Molly herself had been powerless to ease Alix's disappointment at not being able to conceive. How could she possibly ensure the welfare of a baby?

Life wasn't about protection, she'd realized when she saw the dog pounded by the wave, but connection. Only to connect, that's all that was required.

"I want to raise a child with you," she sobbed into Alix's neck.

Alix pulled back to look at her. "Don't do this to me if you're not sure." A hint of the coldness there, ready as a veil just in case.

"I'm sure." Molly looked right back into Alix's

determined eyes, usually so blue but today flavored by the gray of the water. *Sure* may not have been the exact word, but it would have to do.


As she followed the Volvo back to the Valley, Molly thought of her aunts, how they clutched her to them, made such a fuss over her because she was family. She had never felt connected to them, to anything, really. She would have preferred to have come from somewhere with a history, or to have her life shaped by the land, by forces outside herself. But she understood now that her family had shaped her as surely as any natural landscape, wind over sand, water over rock.

She understood now her aunts' sense of entitlement. And she realized that Alix had that same claim on her, as much if not more because they had chosen each other, had not been arbitrarily born into their relationship.

New York wouldn't be home anymore. When they went to visit they could stay with friends, or in a hotel. Her connection to the city had been broken that first night in Miami when she heard Ben's news. That evening, one end of her life had flown up into the air like a kid's lost balloon — the balloon sailing up over the trees, its broken string trailing around her wrist. Devastated, Molly followed its flight, not understanding how something so tragic could happen. She had only just begun to sense the wonder of it. And the exhilarating freedom. It had once been attached to her, now it was free. And now she was free.

• • • • •

They kept Annie outside. They'd wash off the
sand and salt later. For now they shucked their
clothes and jumped into bed to properly restart the
day. When she moved her fingers inside Alix, Molly
was home, and when Alix touched her, that was
home too.

# MONTHS LATER

# *Alix*

I thought I knew what this was going to be like. Once again, I didn't know anything.

I looked "Claire" up in one of those name-your-baby books. It comes from "Clara," meaning bright, shining. And she is the light of our lives, a purifying light. I can come home from a job all tense and Molly will pass the baby to me and it's like wringing out a washcloth, everything just goes and all I'm left with is this joy and love.

I hate how hokey I feel about her, and I don't talk about it with anyone but Molly. Not even my mother. With her I just swap stories, and she's amazed how like me Claire is. When she started eating baby food I gave her spinach and she hated it.

"Now she spits out anything green," I told my mother.

"That's just what you did, dear. Isn't she cute?"

Claire's washed away any conflict there. No trace of chill.

When I was trying to get pregnant and Molly and I argued about Baby, Molly claimed my allegiance would no longer be to her. "If the three of us were in a sinking boat," she'd challenge, "who would you save, me or the baby?" I hated it when she got like that. I'd try silence, but she'd persevere. "The baby, wouldn't you? You'd go for the baby."

"A baby couldn't take care of itself," I'd say. "I know you can take care of yourself."

"But in this situation, we're both in trouble, me and the baby."

"Molly, this argument is academic. Plus, I'm not even pregnant. What's your point?"

"My point is, where will I fit in?"

"Where you always do, right beside me."

"And where's the baby?"

"Snug between us."

"See," she'd gloat, as if that proved something.

I watch her now with little Claire and it's as if someone else had those fights with me. No time for academic arguments now, we're too busy with feedings and diaper-changing and trying to catch up on sleep.

The other day we sat together while Claire slept in Molly's lap. "So, Moll," I asked, "about that sinking boat."

She covered her face with her free hand. "I was such a jerk sometimes."

"You were. But what about it?"

"Moot point," she said.

"You'd never let me get away with an answer like that."

"Okay." She thought a second. "If they don't have life preservers, we stay away from the water." She kissed my cheek. A little peck, but I knew it was an apology for the years of resistance.

Claire opened her eyes then, looked up at Molly, stared at her for a long time. Molly and I, mesmerized by that gaze, didn't speak. Then Claire smiled — talk about bright and shining — as if she'd gotten the joke, understood its deepest meaning, that we were a family and out to protect each other. For what else can I call her removal of our stress and pain but a kind of protection against the world?

Molly smiled back at Claire, and I smiled at both of them, knowing I wouldn't let either of them drown, would give up my life for either of theirs in a heartbeat.

# MOLLY

Holding the sweet weight in her arms Molly suddenly felt she knew everything and nothing. Images flooded her mind, of New York and school and Michael and Claire and beaches and movies and songs from the sixties and her first slow dance with a boy and double dates and her mother quizzing her for a French test and her first slow dance with a woman and her college graduation with only Ben there, and Ben and his sisters and Jerome's stories and Ben's whistling, and a sudden whiff of honeysuckle around five o'clock on a summer afternoon. Molly understood now why she'd retained all the images, all the memories, why she no longer burned for amnesia. She'd been a camera and repository for stories to tell her daughter, to pass on to her everything the world offered, good and bad, for it all belonged.

Molly had dreamed the night before of the touch football game she'd played with her mother and Michael and Ben. The location had been changed to a beach like the one outside Ben's new condo, a soft Miami beach, its shoreline bordered with shells. A slow motion dream: Michael tossed the frisbee to her and it sailed, floated over sand. As she stood poised to catch it the four of them were joined by Alix and the baby, and Jerome, too, while the aunts watched from the sidelines. And her Aunt Rita was there, and all the uncles who had died, and her grandparents. Alix's family joined them, too, and all their friends. The game continued indefinitely, accommodating all who showed up. Suspended in time, they played forever — in silence, protected from everything, the players and spectators guaranteed eternal life by Molly and Alix and their baby and the home they made for her.

Molly looked into the sleeping face of her daughter. *I have so much to tell you.*

But instead of words, all that came out, or bubbled up from somewhere deep in her memory, was of all things a lullaby she'd learned in her fourth grade French class about an owl in an oak tree in the forest.

Molly smiled. She wasn't thinking about safety now, but about this moment. If she had left, she'd miss the moments to come, the ones that string together to become years and memories.

A few of the publications of
**THE NAIAD PRESS, INC.**
P.O. Box 10543 • Tallahassee, Florida 32302
Phone (904) 539-5965
Toll-Free Order Number: 1-800-533-1973
*Mail orders welcome. Please include 15% postage.*

SMOKEY O by Celia Cohen. 176 pp. Relationships on the playing field.
ISBN 1-56280-057-4    $9.95

KATHLEEN O'DONALD by Penny Hayes. 256 pp. Rose and Kathleen find each other and employment in 1909 NYC.
ISBN 1-56280-070-1    9.95

STAYING HOME by Elisabeth Nonas. 256 pp. Molly and Alix want a baby . . . or do they?
ISBN 1-56280-076-0    10.95

TRUE LOVE by Jennifer Fulton. 240 pp. Six lesbians searching for love in all the "right" places.
ISBN 1-56280-035-3    9.95

GARDENIAS WHERE THERE ARE NONE by Molleen Zanger. 176 pp. Why is Melanie inextricably drawn to the old house?
ISBN 1-56280-056-6    9.95

MICHAELA by Sarah Aldridge. 256 pp. A "Sarah Aldridge" romance.
ISBN 1-56280-055-8    10.95

KEEPING SECRETS by Penny Mickelbury. 208 pp. A Gianna Maglione Mystery. First in a series.
ISBN 1-56280-052-3    9.95

THE ROMANTIC NAIAD edited by Katherine V. Forrest & Barbara Grier. 336 pp. Love stories by Naiad Press women.
ISBN 1-56280-054-X    14.95

UNDER MY SKIN by Jaye Maiman. 336 pp. A Robin Miller mystery. 3rd in a series.
ISBN 1-56280-049-3.    10.95

STAY TOONED by Rhonda Dicksion. 144 pp. Cartoons — 1st collection since *Lesbian Survival Manual.*
ISBN 1-56280-045-0    9.95

CAR POOL by Karin Kallmaker. 272pp. Lesbians on wheels and then some!
ISBN 1-56280-048-5    9.95

NOT TELLING MOTHER: STORIES FROM A LIFE by Diane Salvatore. 176 pp. Her 3rd novel.
ISBN 1-56280-044-2    9.95

GOBLIN MARKET by Lauren Wright Douglas. 240pp. A Caitlin Reece Mystery. 5th in a series.
ISBN 1-56280-047-7    9.95

LONG GOODBYES by Nikki Baker. 256 pp. A Virginia Kelly mystery. 3rd in a series.
ISBN 1-56280-042-6    9.95

FRIENDS AND LOVERS by Jackie Calhoun. 224 pp. Mid-western
Lesbian lives and loves. ISBN 1-56280-041-8     9.95

THE CAT CAME BACK by Hilary Mullins. 208 pp. Highly praised
Lesbian novel. ISBN 1-56280-040-X     9.95

BEHIND CLOSED DOORS by Robbi Sommers. 192 pp. Hot, erotic
short stories. ISBN 1-56280-039-6     9.95

CLAIRE OF THE MOON by Nicole Conn. 192 pp. See the movie —
read the book! ISBN 1-56280-038-8     10.95

SILENT HEART by Claire McNab. 192 pp. Exotic Lesbian
romance. ISBN 1-56280-036-1     9.95

HAPPY ENDINGS by Kate Brandt. 272 pp. Intimate conversations
with Lesbian authors. ISBN 1-56280-050-7     10.95

THE SPY IN QUESTION by Amanda Kyle Williams. 256 pp. 4th
Madison McGuire. ISBN 1-56280-037-X     9.95

SAVING GRACE by Jennifer Fulton. 240 pp. Adventure and
romantic entanglement. ISBN 1-56280-051-5     9.95

THE YEAR SEVEN by Molleen Zanger. 208 pp. Women surviving
in a new world. ISBN 1-56280-034-5     9.95

CURIOUS WINE by Katherine V. Forrest. 176 pp. Tenth
Anniversary Edition. The most popular contemporary Lesbian
love story. ISBN 1-56280-053-1     9.95

CHAUTAUQUA by Catherine Ennis. 192 pp. Exciting, romantic
adventure. ISBN 1-56280-032-9     9.95

A PROPER BURIAL by Pat Welch. 192 pp. A Helen Black
mystery. 3rd in a series. ISBN 1-56280-033-7     9.95

SILVERLAKE HEAT: A Novel of Suspense by Carol Schmidt.
240 pp. Rhonda is as hot as Laney's dreams. ISBN 1-56280-031-0     9.95

LOVE, ZENA BETH by Diane Salvatore. 224 pp. The most talked
about lesbian novel of the nineties! ISBN 1-56280-030-2     9.95

A DOORYARD FULL OF FLOWERS by Isabel Miller. 160 pp.
Stories incl. 2 sequels to *Patience and Sarah*. ISBN 1-56280-029-9     9.95

MURDER BY TRADITION by Katherine V. Forrest. 288 pp. A
Kate Delafield Mystery. 4th in a series. ISBN 1-56280-002-7     9.95

THE EROTIC NAIAD edited by Katherine V. Forrest & Barbara Grier.
224 pp. Love stories by Naiad Press authors. ISBN 1-56280-026-4     12.95

DEAD CERTAIN by Claire McNab. 224 pp. A Carol Ashton
mystery. 5th in a series. ISBN 1-56280-027-2     9.95

CRAZY FOR LOVING by Jaye Maiman. 320 pp. A Robin Miller
mystery. 2nd in a series. ISBN 1-56280-025-6     9.95

STONEHURST by Barbara Johnson. 176 pp. Passionate regency
romance. ISBN 1-56280-024-8     9.95

INTRODUCING AMANDA VALENTINE by Rose Beecham.
256 pp. An Amanda Valentine Mystery. First in a series.
ISBN 1-56280-021-3    9.95

UNCERTAIN COMPANIONS by Robbi Sommers. 204 pp.
Steamy, erotic novel.    ISBN 1-56280-017-5    9.95

A TIGER'S HEART by Lauren W. Douglas. 240 pp. A Caitlin
Reece mystery. 4th in a series.    ISBN 1-56280-018-3    9.95

PAPERBACK ROMANCE by Karin Kallmaker. 256 pp. A
delicious romance.    ISBN 1-56280-019-1    9.95

MORTON RIVER VALLEY by Lee Lynch. 304 pp. Lee Lynch at
her best!    ISBN 1-56280-016-7    9.95

THE LAVENDER HOUSE MURDER by Nikki Baker. 224 pp. A
Virginia Kelly Mystery. 2nd in a series.    ISBN 1-56280-012-4    9.95

PASSION BAY by Jennifer Fulton. 224 pp. Passionate romance,
virgin beaches, tropical skies.    ISBN 1-56280-028-0    9.95

STICKS AND STONES by Jackie Calhoun. 208 pp. Contemporary
lesbian lives and loves.    ISBN 1-56280-020-5    9.95

DELIA IRONFOOT by Jeane Harris. 192 pp. Adventure for Delia
and Beth in the Utah mountains.    ISBN 1-56280-014-0    9.95

UNDER THE SOUTHERN CROSS by Claire McNab. 192 pp.
Romantic nights Down Under.    ISBN 1-56280-011-6    9.95

RIVERFINGER WOMEN by Elana Nachman/Dykewomon.
208 pp. Classic Lesbian/feminist novel.    ISBN 1-56280-013-2    8.95

A CERTAIN DISCONTENT by Cleve Boutell. 240 pp. A unique
coterie of women.    ISBN 1-56280-009-4    9.95

GRASSY FLATS by Penny Hayes. 256 pp. Lesbian romance in
the '30s.    ISBN 1-56280-010-8    9.95

A SINGULAR SPY by Amanda K. Williams. 192 pp. 3rd Madison
McGuire.    ISBN 1-56280-008-6    8.95

THE END OF APRIL by Penny Sumner. 240 pp. A Victoria Cross
Mystery. First in a series.    ISBN 1-56280-007-8    8.95

A FLIGHT OF ANGELS by Sarah Aldridge. 240 pp. Romance set at
the National Gallery of Art    ISBN 1-56280-001-9    9.95

HOUSTON TOWN by Deborah Powell. 208 pp. A Hollis Carpenter
mystery. Second in a series.    ISBN 1-56280-006-X    8.95

KISS AND TELL by Robbi Sommers. 192 pp. Scorching stories by
the author of *Pleasures*.    ISBN 1-56280-005-1    9.95

STILL WATERS by Pat Welch. 208 pp. A Helen Black mystery.
2nd in a series.    ISBN 0-941483-97-5    9.95

TO LOVE AGAIN by Evelyn Kennedy. 208 pp. Wildly
romantic love story.    ISBN 0-941483-85-1    9.95

IN THE GAME by Nikki Baker. 192 pp. A Virginia Kelly
mystery. First in a series.              ISBN 1-56280-004-3        9.95

AVALON by Mary Jane Jones. 256 pp. A Lesbian Arthurian
romance.                                 ISBN 0-941483-96-7        9.95

STRANDED by Camarin Grae. 320 pp. Entertaining, riveting
adventure.                               ISBN 0-941483-99-1        9.95

THE DAUGHTERS OF ARTEMIS by Lauren Wright Douglas.
240 pp. A Caitlin Reece mystery. 3rd in a series.
                                         ISBN 0-941483-95-9        9.95

CLEARWATER by Catherine Ennis. 176 pp. Romantic secrets
of a small Louisiana town.               ISBN 0-941483-65-7        8.95

THE HALLELUJAH MURDERS by Dorothy Tell. 176 pp. A Poppy
Dillworth mystery. 2nd in a series.      ISBN 0-941483-88-6        8.95

ZETA BASE by Judith Alguire. 208 pp. Lesbian triangle
on a future Earth.                       ISBN 0-941483-94-0        9.95

SECOND CHANCE by Jackie Calhoun. 256 pp. Contemporary
Lesbian lives and loves.                 ISBN 0-941483-93-2        9.95

BENEDICTION by Diane Salvatore. 272 pp. Striking,
contemporary romantic novel.             ISBN 0-941483-90-8        9.95

CALLING RAIN by Karen Marie Christa Minns. 240 pp.
Spellbinding, erotic love story          ISBN 0-941483-87-8        9.95

BLACK IRIS by Jeane Harris. 192 pp. Caroline's hidden past . . .
                                         ISBN 0-941483-68-1        8.95

TOUCHWOOD by Karin Kallmaker. 240 pp. Loving, May/
December romance.                        ISBN 0-941483-76-2        9.95

BAYOU CITY SECRETS by Deborah Powell. 224 pp. A Hollis
Carpenter mystery. First in a series.    ISBN 0-941483-91-6        9.95

COP OUT by Claire McNab. 208 pp. A Carol Ashton mystery.
4th in a series.                         ISBN 0-941483-84-3        9.95

LODESTAR by Phyllis Horn. 224 pp. Romantic, fast-moving
adventure.                               ISBN 0-941483-83-5        8.95

THE BEVERLY MALIBU by Katherine V. Forrest. 288 pp. A
Kate Delafield Mystery. 3rd in a series. ISBN 0-941483-48-7        9.95

THAT OLD STUDEBAKER by Lee Lynch. 272 pp. Andy's affair
with Regina and her attachment to her beloved car.
                                         ISBN 0-941483-82-7        9.95

PASSION'S LEGACY by Lori Paige. 224 pp. Sarah is swept into
the arms of Augusta Pym in this delightful historical romance.
                                         ISBN 0-941483-81-9        8.95

THE PROVIDENCE FILE by Amanda Kyle Williams. 256 pp.
Second Madison McGuire                   ISBN 0-941483-92-4        8.95

I LEFT MY HEART by Jaye Maiman. 320 pp. A Robin Miller
Mystery. First in a series.                    ISBN 0-941483-72-X      9.95

THE PRICE OF SALT by Patricia Highsmith (writing as Claire
Morgan). 288 pp. Classic lesbian novel, first issued in 1952 . . .
acknowledged by its author under her own, very famous, name.
                                               ISBN 1-56280-003-5      9.95

SIDE BY SIDE by Isabel Miller. 256 pp. From beloved author of
*Patience and Sarah*.                          ISBN 0-941483-77-0      9.95

STAYING POWER: LONG TERM LESBIAN COUPLES
by Susan E. Johnson. 352 pp. Joys of coupledom.
                                               ISBN 0-941-483-75-4    12.95

SLICK by Camarin Grae. 304 pp. Exotic, erotic adventure.
                                               ISBN 0-941483-74-6      9.95

NINTH LIFE by Lauren Wright Douglas. 256 pp. A Caitlin
Reece mystery. 2nd in a series.        ISBN 0-941483-50-9      8.95

PLAYERS by Robbi Sommers. 192 pp. Sizzling, erotic novel.
                                               ISBN 0-941483-73-8      9.95

MURDER AT RED ROOK RANCH by Dorothy Tell. 224 pp.
A Poppy Dillworth mystery. 1st in a series.    ISBN 0-941483-80-0      8.95

LESBIAN SURVIVAL MANUAL by Rhonda Dicksion.
112 pp. Cartoons!                              ISBN 0-941483-71-1      8.95

A ROOM FULL OF WOMEN by Elisabeth Nonas. 256 pp.
Contemporary Lesbian lives.            ISBN 0-941483-69-X      9.95

PRIORITIES by Lynda Lyons 288 pp. Science fiction with
a twist.                                       ISBN 0-941483-66-5      8.95

THEME FOR DIVERSE INSTRUMENTS by Jane Rule. 208
pp. Powerful romantic lesbian stories.         ISBN 0-941483-63-0      8.95

LESBIAN QUERIES by Hertz & Ertman. 112 pp. The questions
you were too embarrassed to ask.               ISBN 0-941483-67-3      8.95

CLUB 12 by Amanda Kyle Williams. 288 pp. Espionage thriller
featuring a lesbian agent!                     ISBN 0-941483-64-9      8.95

DEATH DOWN UNDER by Claire McNab. 240 pp. A Carol
Ashton mystery. 3rd in a series.               ISBN 0-941483-39-8      9.95

MONTANA FEATHERS by Penny Hayes. 256 pp. Vivian and
Elizabeth find love in frontier Montana.       ISBN 0-941483-61-4      8.95

CHESAPEAKE PROJECT by Phyllis Horn. 304 pp. Jessie &
Meredith in perilous adventure.                ISBN 0-941483-58-4      8.95

LIFESTYLES by Jackie Calhoun. 224 pp. Contemporary Lesbian
lives and loves.                               ISBN 0-941483-57-6      9.95

VIRAGO by Karen Marie Christa Minns. 208 pp. Darsen has
chosen Ginny.                                  ISBN 0-941483-56-8      8.95

WILDERNESS TREK by Dorothy Tell. 192 pp. Six women on
vacation learning "new" skills. ISBN 0-941483-60-6    8.95

MURDER BY THE BOOK by Pat Welch. 256 pp. A Helen
Black Mystery. First in a series. ISBN 0-941483-59-2    9.95

LESBIANS IN GERMANY by Lillian Faderman & B. Eriksson.
128 pp. Fiction, poetry, essays. ISBN 0-941483-62-2    8.95

THERE'S SOMETHING I'VE BEEN MEANING TO TELL
YOU Ed. by Loralee MacPike. 288 pp. Gay men and lesbians
coming out to their children. ISBN 0-941483-44-4    9.95

LIFTING BELLY by Gertrude Stein. Ed. by Rebecca Mark. 104
pp. Erotic poetry. ISBN 0-941483-51-7    8.95

ROSE PENSKI by Roz Perry. 192 pp. Adult lovers in a long-term
relationship. ISBN 0-941483-37-1    8.95

AFTER THE FIRE by Jane Rule. 256 pp. Warm, human novel
by this incomparable author. ISBN 0-941483-45-2    8.95

SUE SLATE, PRIVATE EYE by Lee Lynch. 176 pp. The gay
folk of Peacock Alley are *all cats*. ISBN 0-941483-52-5    8.95

CHRIS by Randy Salem. 224 pp. Golden oldie. Handsome Chris
and her adventures. ISBN 0-941483-42-8    8.95

THREE WOMEN by March Hastings. 232 pp. Golden oldie. A
triangle among wealthy sophisticates. ISBN 0-941483-43-6    8.95

RICE AND BEANS by Valeria Taylor. 232 pp. Love and
romance on poverty row. ISBN 0-941483-41-X    8.95

PLEASURES by Robbi Sommers. 204 pp. Unprecedented
eroticism. ISBN 0-941483-49-5    8.95

EDGEWISE by Camarin Grae. 372 pp. Spellbinding
adventure. ISBN 0-941483-19-3    9.95

FATAL REUNION by Claire McNab. 224 pp. A Carol Ashton
mystery. 2nd in a series. ISBN 0-941483-40-1    8.95

KEEP TO ME STRANGER by Sarah Aldridge. 372 pp. Romance
set in a department store dynasty. ISBN 0-941483-38-X    9.95

IN THE BLOOD by Lauren Wright Douglas. 252 pp. Lesbian
science fiction adventure fantasy ISBN 0-941483-22-3    8.95

THE BEE'S KISS by Shirley Verel. 216 pp. Delicate, delicious
romance. ISBN 0-941483-36-3    8.95

RAGING MOTHER MOUNTAIN by Pat Emmerson. 264 pp.
Furosa Firechild's adventures in Wonderland. ISBN 0-941483-35-5    8.95

IN EVERY PORT by Karin Kallmaker. 228 pp. Jessica's sexy,
adventuresome travels. ISBN 0-941483-37-7    9.95

OF LOVE AND GLORY by Evelyn Kennedy. 192 pp. Exciting
WWII romance. ISBN 0-941483-32-0 8.95

CLICKING STONES by Nancy Tyler Glenn. 288 pp. Love
transcending time. ISBN 0-941483-31-2 9.95

SURVIVING SISTERS by Gail Pass. 252 pp. Powerful love
story. ISBN 0-941483-16-9 8.95

SOUTH OF THE LINE by Catherine Ennis. 216 pp. Civil War
adventure. ISBN 0-941483-29-0 8.95

WOMAN PLUS WOMAN by Dolores Klaich. 300 pp. Supurb
Lesbian overview. ISBN 0-941483-28-2 9.95

HEAVY GILT by Dolores Klaich. 192 pp. Lesbian detective/
disappearing homophobes/upper class gay society.
ISBN 0-941483-25-8 8.95

THE FINER GRAIN by Denise Ohio. 216 pp. Brilliant young
college lesbian novel. ISBN 0-941483-11-8 8.95

HIGH CONTRAST by Jessie Lattimore. 264 pp. Women of the
Crystal Palace. ISBN 0-941483-17-7 8.95

OCTOBER OBSESSION by Meredith More. Josie's rich, secret
Lesbian life. ISBN 0-941483-18-5 8.95

BEFORE STONEWALL: THE MAKING OF A GAY AND
LESBIAN COMMUNITY by Andrea Weiss & Greta Schiller.
96 pp., 25 illus. ISBN 0-941483-20-7 7.95

WE WALK THE BACK OF THE TIGER by Patricia A. Murphy.
192 pp. Romantic Lesbian novel/beginning women's movement.
ISBN 0-941483-13-4 8.95

SUNDAY'S CHILD by Joyce Bright. 216 pp. Lesbian athletics, at
last the novel about sports. ISBN 0-941483-12-6 8.95

OSTEN'S BAY by Zenobia N. Vole. 204 pp. Sizzling adventure
romance set on Bonaire. ISBN 0-941483-15-0 8.95

LESSONS IN MURDER by Claire McNab. 216 pp. A Carol
Ashton mystery. First in a series. ISBN 0-941483-14-2 9.95

YELLOWTHROAT by Penny Hayes. 240 pp. Margarita, bandit,
kidnaps Julia. ISBN 0-941483-10-X 8.95

SAPPHISTRY: THE BOOK OF LESBIAN SEXUALITY by
Pat Califia. 3d edition, revised. 208 pp. ISBN 0-941483-24-X 10.95

CHERISHED LOVE by Evelyn Kennedy. 192 pp. Erotic
Lesbian love story. ISBN 0-941483-08-8 9.95

LAST SEPTEMBER by Helen R. Hull. 208 pp. Six stories & a
glorious novella. ISBN 0-941483-09-6 8.95

THE SECRET IN THE BIRD by Camarin Grae. 312 pp. Striking,
psychological suspense novel. ISBN 0-941483-05-3 8.95

TO THE LIGHTNING by Catherine Ennis. 208 pp. Romantic
Lesbian 'Robinson Crusoe' adventure.          ISBN 0-941483-06-1      8.95

THE OTHER SIDE OF VENUS by Shirley Verel. 224 pp.
Luminous, romantic love story.                ISBN 0-941483-07-X      8.95

DREAMS AND SWORDS by Katherine V. Forrest. 192 pp.
Romantic, erotic, imaginative stories.        ISBN 0-941483-03-7      8.95

MEMORY BOARD by Jane Rule. 336 pp. Memorable novel
about an aging Lesbian couple.                ISBN 0-941483-02-9      9.95

THE ALWAYS ANONYMOUS BEAST by Lauren Wright
Douglas. 224 pp. A Caitlin Reece mystery. First in a series.
                                              ISBN 0-941483-04-5      8.95

DUSTY'S QUEEN OF HEARTS DINER by Lee Lynch. 240 pp.
Romantic blue-collar novel.                   ISBN 0-941483-01-0      8.95

PARENTS MATTER by Ann Muller. 240 pp. Parents'
relationships with Lesbian daughters and gay sons.
                                              ISBN 0-930044-91-6      9.95

MAGDALENA by Sarah Aldridge. 352 pp. Epic Lesbian novel
set on three continents.                      ISBN 0-930044-99-1      8.95

THE BLACK AND WHITE OF IT by Ann Allen Shockley.
144 pp. Short stories.                        ISBN 0-930044-96-7      7.95

SAY JESUS AND COME TO ME by Ann Allen Shockley. 288
pp. Contemporary romance.                     ISBN 0-930044-98-3      8.95

LOVING HER by Ann Allen Shockley. 192 pp. Romantic love
story.                                        ISBN 0-930044-97-5      7.95

MURDER AT THE NIGHTWOOD BAR by Katherine V.
Forrest. 240 pp. A Kate Delafield mystery. Second in a series.
                                              ISBN 0-930044-92-4      9.95

ZOE'S BOOK by Gail Pass. 224 pp. Passionate, obsessive love
story.                                        ISBN 0-930044-95-9      7.95

WINGED DANCER by Camarin Grae. 228 pp. Erotic Lesbian
adventure story.                              ISBN 0-930044-88-6      8.95

PAZ by Camarin Grae. 336 pp. Romantic Lesbian adventurer
with the power to change the world.           ISBN 0-930044-89-4      8.95

SOUL SNATCHER by Camarin Grae. 224 pp. A puzzle, an
adventure, a mystery — Lesbian romance.       ISBN 0-930044-90-8      8.95

THE LOVE OF GOOD WOMEN by Isabel Miller. 224 pp.
Long-awaited new novel by the author of the beloved *Patience
and Sarah.*                                   ISBN 0-930044-81-9      8.95

THE HOUSE AT PELHAM FALLS by Brenda Weathers. 240
pp. Suspenseful Lesbian ghost story.          ISBN 0-930044-79-7      7.95

HOME IN YOUR HANDS by Lee Lynch. 240 pp. More stories
from the author of *Old Dyke Tales.*          ISBN 0-930044-80-0      7.95

SURPLUS by Sylvia Stevenson. 342 pp. A classic early Lesbian
novel.                                      ISBN 0-930044-78-9      7.95

PEMBROKE PARK by Michelle Martin. 256 pp. Derring-do
and daring romance in Regency England.      ISBN 0-930044-77-0      7.95

THE LONG TRAIL by Penny Hayes. 248 pp. Vivid adventures
of two women in love in the old west.       ISBN 0-930044-76-2      8.95

AN EMERGENCE OF GREEN by Katherine V. Forrest. 288
pp. Powerful novel of sexual discovery.     ISBN 0-930044-69-X      9.95

THE LESBIAN PERIODICALS INDEX edited by Claire
Potter. 432 pp. Author & subject index.     ISBN 0-930044-74-6     12.95

DESERT OF THE HEART by Jane Rule. 224 pp. A classic;
basis for the movie *Desert Hearts*.        ISBN 0-930044-73-8      9.95

FOR KEEPS by Elisabeth Nonas. 144 pp. Contemporary novel
about losing and finding love.              ISBN 0-930044-71-1      7.95

TORCHLIGHT TO VALHALLA by Gale Wilhelm. 128 pp.
Classic novel by a great Lesbian writer.    ISBN 0-930044-68-1      7.95

LESBIAN NUNS: BREAKING SILENCE edited by Rosemary
Curb and Nancy Manahan. 432 pp. Unprecedented autobiographies
of religious life.                          ISBN 0-930044-62-2      9.95

THE SWASHBUCKLER by Lee Lynch. 288 pp. Colorful novel
set in Greenwich Village in the sixties.    ISBN 0-930044-66-5      8.95

MISFORTUNE'S FRIEND by Sarah Aldridge. 320 pp. Histori-
cal Lesbian novel set on two continents.    ISBN 0-930044-67-3      7.95

SEX VARIANT WOMEN IN LITERATURE by Jeannette
Howard Foster. 448 pp. Literary history.    ISBN 0-930044-65-7      8.95

A HOT-EYED MODERATE by Jane Rule. 252 pp. Hard-hitting
essays on gay life; writing; art.           ISBN 0-930044-57-6      7.95

WE TOO ARE DRIFTING by Gale Wilhelm. 128 pp. Timeless
Lesbian novel, a masterpiece.               ISBN 0-930044-61-4      6.95

AMATEUR CITY by Katherine V. Forrest. 224 pp. A Kate
Delafield mystery. First in a series.       ISBN 0-930044-55-X      9.95

THE SOPHIE HOROWITZ STORY by Sarah Schulman. 176
pp. Engaging novel of madcap intrigue.      ISBN 0-930044-54-1      7.95

THE YOUNG IN ONE ANOTHER'S ARMS by Jane Rule.
224 pp. Classic Jane Rule.                  ISBN 0-930044-53-3      9.95

OLD DYKE TALES by Lee Lynch. 224 pp. Extraordinary
stories of our diverse Lesbian lives.       ISBN 0-930044-51-7      8.95

DAUGHTERS OF A CORAL DAWN by Katherine V. Forrest.
240 pp. Novel set in a Lesbian new world.   ISBN 0-930044-50-9      9.95

AGAINST THE SEASON by Jane Rule. 224 pp. Luminous,
complex novel of interrelationships.        ISBN 0-930044-48-7      8.95